I0667362

YOURS TO TREASURE

LANTERN BAY, BOOK 2

SOPHIE HAYDON

BAY BOOKS

Yours to Treasure
by Sophie Haydon

A celebrity chef returning home to face her past mistakes, a principled ex-rugby player who wants a life away from the spotlight, and a heartbreaking secret which threatens to tear them apart...

—The Mackenzies—
A Place Called Home
Secrets at Parata Bay
Escape to Shelter Springs
What you See in the Stars
Second Chance at Whisper Creek
Summer at the Lakehouse Café

—Lantern Bay—
Yours to Give
Yours to Treasure
Yours to Cherish
Yours to Keep
Yours Forever
Yours to Love

For more information about this author, visit:
https://sophiehaydon.com

© 2017 Diana Fraser

ISBN: 978-1-927323-48-9 (epub)
ISBN: 978-1-991021-14-4 (2022 Amazon Print Edn)
ISBN: 978-1-991021-31-1 (2022 Draft2Digital Print Edn)

CONTENTS

"Love is not consolation. It is light."
— **Simone Weil**

---

*R*achel Connelly placed her jandal-clad feet either side of the dried arrangement which her father liked to call a 'dormant' camellia shrub, and gripped it as close to the base as possible. She gave a small tug to test. Nothing. This sucker was tougher than it looked. She took a deep breath and shifted her weight from foot to foot, gaining a more secure stance. Then she gripped it lower down and gave a short, sharp tug. It came away easily—too easily, Rachel thought with a small cry, as she found herself flat on her backside on the grass.

"Hey!" a voice called through the woods. "Are you okay?"

She turned to see runner's shoes and legs—strong, brown, hairy legs—running up to her through the small copse of trees which lay between the house and the road. She twisted onto her stomach and looked up, at the same time as the knees bobbed down and a concerned face came into view. A strangely familiar face.

"I'm fine," she said, trying, but not succeeding, to place the face. Another glance at the face and the familiarity receded. She definitely didn't know this man.

"Here." He reached out and placed a large hand under her upper arm. "Let me help you up."

Before Rachel could reply, the hand lifted her as if she were a feather. She definitely *wasn't* a feather.

"Oh! Well, thank you." She slowly looked up, past running shorts and a sleeveless t-shirt which revealed a body that was built. *Really* built. She didn't know whether her gasp was audible or not, but by the looks of his grin, she suspected it was.

He ducked his head to inspect her face. "You sure you're okay?"

"Yes, it was only a tumble." She waved around the dead shrub she was still holding, unable to move her gaze from his. "It came away easier than I thought."

He looked at it with a smile. "It would do. It's been dead these past couple of years. Like much of these woods. I've been wondering when someone would do something about it."

"Ah, that someone is my father. And he's still not convinced anything needs doing."

"You're one of the Connellys, then?"

"Yes. Rachel Connelly."

He stuck out his hand. "Pleased to meet you. I'm Zane Black."

She frowned. The instant she'd seen him she'd thought she'd known him, but she didn't. His name wasn't familiar and she was sure she wouldn't have forgotten someone like him.

She took hold of his hand and it felt good—big, strong, and yet gentle. It didn't grip you as if it was trying to make you submit, trying to make you aware of how strong he was. There was obviously no need for that.

"Good to meet you, Zane. You live round here?"

"Yeah, in the next valley. Up from Ti Tahi Bay."

There was a small flutter in her stomach. *Ti Tahi.* It sent memories flooding back of the time when she was only barely out of childhood and anxious to become an adult—a sexual adult.

"Ti Tahi," she repeated.

"Yeah. It's up in the hills near here. It's a small community built around a meeting house. My ancestors have lived on the land for centuries. It's steeped in history."

You bet it is, she thought. Including mine. "Yes, I know where it is."

"You do? Have you met my family?"

"No. Never. At least I don't think I have." She'd only known the boy who'd taken her virginity. She'd never met his family.

"I've seen you before." He suddenly looked unsure, as if he suspected he'd said too much.

"Where?" Surely she wouldn't forget someone as striking as him?

He looked around as if hoping someone would rescue him. There was no one. He turned back to her. "Oh, around."

"You like cooking?" she asked. Most people recognized her from her shows.

He shrugged and looked even more confused if that was possible. "Why?"

"Just wondered... about where you might have seen me before."

"Ah," he said, but didn't elaborate.

"Rachel?" A voice came from the house behind them. She turned and saw her father, Jim Connelly, waving at her. "Amber's been trying to reach you on the phone!"

"Okay!" she called, retrieving the quietly vibrating phone from where she'd left it, perched on a mostly empty wheelbarrow. "Excuse me," she muttered to Zane. "Hello?" She half-turned away. "Amber! Hi! Yes, sure, I'll be at the café mid-afternoon at the latest. See you then." She smiled as Amber made kissing noises down the phone. She finished the call and glanced up to see a pair of interested eyes quickly look away.

"I'd better go," said Rachel. "Things to do… Places to go…" She smiled uncertainly, feeling uncomfortable standing so close to this giant of a man who was clad only in brief shorts and t-shirt, exposing dark skin and a muscled body. Stunning, she thought, trying to keep her gaze away from his body, and focused on his face. Trouble was, that was impressive, too, in an uncompromising kind of way.

"Sure." He grinned and his face lit up, softening his features and revealing perfect teeth. He looked like a different man. He took a few steps back and indicated the garden. "Go easy on the weeding."

She nodded, and tossed the dead shrub into the wheelbarrow, feeling unaccountably shy. He turned away and began to jog back to the road. "See you," said Rachel impulsively. Some urge made her want to say something more to him, to keep the connection going.

"Yeah." He turned and grinned again. "You will."

Rachel walked away, determined not to be caught watching him run along the road. She paused beside a tree. He wouldn't notice now if she took a peek. She turned and soaked up the view of this tall, broad-shouldered man, running. It was the kind of jog which professional athletes do, the body powerful, contained, as if the effort were nothing, his arms and legs pumping with precision and total control. He looked like he could control anything. The thought made her go weak at the knees. At that moment he was about to round the bend and he turned and caught her staring at him. He grinned, a very masculine satisfied grin, waved and was gone before she could say, "caught red-handed."

"Dad?" she called out, as she walked up to the house. He'd disappeared again. He disappeared every time she tried to sort out the garden. He'd always hated gardening, and it had to be said, he was particularly bad at it, and had always left it to his wife to do. But it had been six years since she'd died and everything was going from bad to worse. What was once charming, had now become dilapidated.

"Dad?" she called out again, as she walked up the steps to Belendroit. She looked around and then heard him. He was standing with his back to her, looking out across the bay, one of the old lanterns after which their bay had been named, jutting out from the house beside him. He was holding a phone and obviously intent on listening to every word. He suddenly guffawed with laughter. "Absolutely right, Laura, my darling. And if that ever happens again, you know exactly what to say to him." He laughed again and then farewelled the newest member of the family.

"Darling!" he exclaimed, as he replaced the phone. "You'll never guess who that was!" Her father always spoke as if he were on a stage. He'd multiplied the family inheritance through his financial investments but his first love had always been the theatre.

"Laura?"

"Yes! She rang to tell me what she and Max have been up to." He laughed at the memory of the conversation. "You'll never believe—"

Rachel placed her aching butt into a chair and poured herself a glass of lemonade. Her father's stories were notoriously long, often taking longer to describe than the actual incident itself. But this time she was interested in hearing about Laura's latest exploit. Seemed marriage to her big brother, Max, hadn't slowed her down in the least. She might have re-focused her energies into a smaller geography and be working alongside Max now, but their lives were pretty much the stuff of legends in the making.

Her father paused and looked at her carefully. "You look tired. I know you're here to sort things out, but you shouldn't exhaust yourself."

"Someone has to," she said pointedly. "That garden needs a good overhaul. Weeding, pruning... and all those other things which people do to gardens. I wish you'd let us hire someone to sort it out."

He took a sip of the lemonade and narrowed his gaze, looking out at the overgrown garden, for all the world like a member of landed gentry inspecting his estate. Which, knowing their family tree, Rachel supposed he was. Maybe looking out at it now, he'd realize the state it was in.

"Wasn't it a wonderful wedding?" He smiled at Rachel and she groaned. His mind was miles away from his surroundings, as usual.

"Yes, Dad, it was." Rachel finished her glass and rose.

"Laura looked gorgeous, didn't she?"

"Of course she did. I don't think there's any other way that Laura could possibly look."

"And Max. I've never seen him happier."

"Yeah." Rachel softened at the thought of Max, remembering how he'd broken down in the hospital when Laura was ill. She'd never seen her big brother so distraught. She'd known then, that he adored Laura.

"I wish *you* would tie the knot."

It was like a punch in the gut. You never knew when it was coming, but it came all right. She jumped up. "Yeah, right, Dad."

She couldn't take this any longer. Somehow, with unerring ability, her father found that small place deep inside her that was raw and hurting. He was right. She'd returned to sort things out. He thought she meant the garden and the house. And she did. But there was more to sort out than those things.

"Where are you going?"

"I told Amber I'd call into the café."

Her father grimaced. "At least she's not allowed to cook in the café. Give her my love. I don't know why she took that tiny house in town when she has a perfectly good room here," he grumbled.

"Maybe because she's twenty and wants to spread her wings?"

"Maybe," he conceded. "But hopefully she'll come back. Just like you have."

"Hopefully, unlike me, she won't have to," Rachel muttered, out of earshot of her father, as she grabbed her bag and headed for the shower. She was done with gardening for the day.

A FEW HOURS later Rachel gunned her red Mini Cooper down the road toward the small town of Akaroa. The roof was down and the sea breeze whipped up her hair. She tried to focus on the beauty around her, on the sun beating down on her head, but her father's words had stirred thoughts she'd prefer to forget.

She parked the car some distance away from the café on purpose. As she walked past the school she glanced in. The school grounds were empty. She usually came later when the kids were on recess.

She swallowed her disappointment and continued on, lost in her thoughts. She glanced back at the school just as she was turning a corner. She stumbled into a wall, or not a wall, she thought as a hand reached out and held her steady.

"Hey, sorry," she said. "I wasn't looking where I was going." Then she looked up. "You!"

Zane Black grinned. "Yeah, me. And no problem. You were too busy looking at the school. Looking for your kid?"

She jumped back. "What? No! I mean, I don't have a kid. I... well..."

"Sorry. I assumed... Anyway, are you okay?"

"Sure." She flexed her wrist, realizing that it hurt most where he'd grabbed her. And looking at his hand, she could see why. It was the size of a dinner plate. She slowly looked up, past casual shorts now, and a different colored t-shirt. He'd obviously showered and changed, luckily not into anything more concealing. It would have been a crime to cover up that body. "So... this is a coincidence."

He cleared his throat and looked briefly embarrassed before looking back at her with a lopsided grin. "Not really. I hear there's a real good café round here."

"Yes, I'm going there. It's where my sister works." It suddenly dawned on her that he'd overheard that much from her phone conversation with Amber. "Ah..." She raised an eyebrow, hesitating. Wasn't she here to avoid all of this? To clear her head of distractions and sort herself out?

"I wondered if you'd like some company? I hear their iced teas are good."

She laughed and glanced again at those broad shoulders and that gorgeous, heart-stopping grin and melting brown eyes, and the answer slipped out of her mouth before she had time to engage her brain. "You know, I think that would be great." His grin broadened. "So, you enjoy iced tea?" she asked, as they walked toward the sea front.

He glanced at her as if she was mad. "Me? No way. Too fancy. Either beer or water."

"Oh!" She didn't think she knew any man whose tastes were so black and white.

"Is that a problem? I guess I'm not the sophisticated type." He stopped walking. "Say so if you don't want to go any further."

She looked up at him and wondered if anyone ever did anything else but agree with him. He was at least six foot four and he spoke with an authority which seemed entirely natural. "We're going for a cup of tea—or water—yes?" She wondered if she'd missed anything. Again that gorgeous grin.

"Sure. Sorry."

They walked in silence to the door of the colonial-style building, with its big windows and high stud which over-looked the road and water, and walked inside.

"Rach!" squealed Amber, as she walked over. She was dressed all in black as was *de rigueur* in the cool café. "You're here at last!" She gave her a big hug and only then looked behind her and her eyebrows rose. "And... you've brought someone." She cocked her head to one side. "And not just anyone. Hello, Zane."

"Hey, Amber, how are you doing?" said Zane, with a smile.

"Good, thanks. Is this a social call or are you here to eat?"

Rachel and Zane's eyes met. "To eat," they both said at the same time. They laughed and Amber looked from one to the other with interest, and showed them to a table by the window.

"I'll fetch some menus while you... relax," she said, smiling at Rachel, "and enjoy the scenery."

Rachel watched Amber walk away and marveled once more at her sweet sister—stunning with her red hair and unencumbered for once by her hippy clothes. She turned to say something to Zane to find him watching her closely. He immediately looked away.

She smiled. "Seems you know everyone around here, except me."

He held her gaze and looked thoughtful. He checked over his shoulder and shifted in his chair, then met her gaze once more, his eyes warmer. "I might not know you, but I've seen you around."

"Really? Where?"

"Oh… around town."

Rachel frowned a little. Around town? Surely she couldn't have met the only person around here who didn't watch her TV show?

"Did I say something wrong?"

"No, not at all. It just feels unnerving when people know me but I don't know them."

"You're not into rugby, then?" He looked up at her with a grin.

Suddenly light dawned and she sat back in her chair. "You're the All Black!" She slapped the palm of her hand against her forehead. "Of course! I've heard about you. How could I have been so dumb?"

"Maybe because you don't follow rugby?"

She laughed. "I'm the only one in my family who doesn't. Probably the only one in my family who wouldn't recognize you. How come you don't play now?"

He tapped one sturdy knee. "Cartilage damage. I could have gone on and had an operation and driven my body into the ground, but there were other things I wanted to do."

She was about to ask what those things were, when her phone buzzed and she took it out of her pocket. She glanced at it, heart sinking, and slid it onto the table away from her.

"Take it if you want."

"No. It's no one I want to speak to."

He glanced at the image which had appeared on the phone. A frown briefly fell onto his broad strong face as she quickly switched off the phone.

"So... what were these other things you wanted to do?" she asked.

"Lead a real life."

His answer was so profound, so unlike the superficial chat she usually had with men, that she was stunned. "That's... that's quite something."

He cocked his head to one side. "Why?"

"Most people, from my experience, want anything *but* real."

"Like what?"

"They want glamor, excitement, sensation." She waved her hands expansively. "Fame and fortune."

"Is that what *you* want?"

It was a question no one had ever asked her before. People always assumed she'd sought out her high profile career for one reason—to be famous—and wished to continue on that path for the same reason.

"I... I'm not sure." She shrugged. "Maybe I did once."

He leaned forward. "And now?"

She felt uncomfortable. This conversation was getting way too serious, way too quickly.

"And now?" She laughed. "I'm here, aren't I? In this backwater, tucked away from the rest of the world. What do you think?"

His face fell. He knew she was avoiding the question and was disappointed by the answer.

"Anyway," she continued. "Where have you seen me before? I'm intrigued."

"I run every day and I've seen you at the house on the point. In the garden. I saw you up a tree once."

"The oak? Yeah, I managed to get one branch chopped, but the rest defeated me."

"And I saw you trying to mend the fence last week. It didn't look like you succeeded."

"No." She grimaced. "I didn't. I only managed to wrench half the wretched piece of rotten timber and got a splinter for my troubles."

"That's no good. You need a man to sort things out."

She bristled. "I don't need a man to do anything of the sort!"

"Well, you don't seem to be doing so well on your own." His voice wasn't accusative, he was merely stating a fact, but his words still rankled.

She took a deep breath. "No, I guess I don't. Sorry, I didn't mean to sound short."

"And I didn't mean to sound like a male chauvinist. I simply meant you needed someone a bit stronger. I'm happy to help."

She sat back in her chair. "I couldn't. I mean that's very kind of you, but we don't know each other."

"You know my name, you know I used to play with the All Blacks, you know where I live, you know I only drink water or beer. What else would you like to know?"

She shrugged. "What do people usually need to know about the other?"

"I'll reel off some stuff and then you can tell me when you know enough about me."

"Okay."

"I work here in Akaroa, as well as on the marae, and for the Ngai Tahu Tribal Council. I'm a straightforward man—I either like things or I don't. Some people have called me black and white, but I prefer to see it as having old-fashioned values and knowing my own mind. Enough?"

"You can carry on if you like." She could have gone on listening to him forever, continued to look into those wonderful dark brown eyes, allowing her gaze to stray over his strong face, sensuous lips and occasionally down to his muscled forearms which rested on the arms of his chair. He was a big man, an impressive man, and definitely a man comfortable in his own skin—from his calm and assured gaze down to his strong body, which was relaxed and at ease.

"The rest you can find out yourself. If you want to, that is."

Again the uncertainty warmed her heart. It had been years since she'd met someone as endearingly uncertain about her as this man.

She smiled, determined to ignore the implication that he wanted to spend time with her. "I think that's enough to be going on with. And, yes, that would be really nice of you, if you could help us out in the woods and garden. It's a mess and beyond me. Dad doesn't seem interested and refuses to allow his sons to work on it, let alone hired strangers. I'd have to clear it with him first."

"Oh, I'm sure Jim will be okay about it. Whenever we've worked on community projects together we've got on fine. I'll come by after work tomorrow."

"You know my dad, too?"

"Of course. Who doesn't know your dad?"

It was a reasonable question, given her father knew everyone in and around Akaroa, not only because he'd spent his whole life there but because he was as nosy as hell, and was a member of any club, any community activity, that was going.

"Hey!" said Amber, suddenly appearing and thrusting menus onto them. "Hope I'm not interrupting anything!"

Rachel looked up feeling strangely guilty. There might not appear to be anything going on, but in her imagination there was, and Amber had obviously sensed it. "Of course not."

"Right, whatever you say." But from her grin, Rachel knew she didn't believe her answer. "So…" continued Amber. "What can I get you? We've some lovely cakes, including some I made." She grinned. "The boss doesn't know, but I reckon we needed some vegan, non-dairy options."

"Thanks, Amber, but I fancy one of those custard squares today."

"Sure. With Earl Grey tea?"

"That would be lovely."

"And for you, Zane?" asked Amber.

"I'll have the usual, thanks."

They grinned at each other.

"You come here often?" asked Rachel.

"I bring my *taua*—my gran—in here when we're in town, along with my sisters sometimes."

"Your gran is so impressive," said Amber. "She has great *mana*, great dignity. And she sorts you guys out like you were five-year-olds."

Zane grinned. "That's my gran. A force to be reckoned with."

"Maybe, but she's always charming to me."

They both watched Amber walk away.

"That's because your sister's sweet," explained Zane.

Rachel felt an unexpected twist in her gut. It was something like jealousy, she thought with surprise. She also hadn't felt *that* in years. She glanced up at lips that weren't full but were definitely sexy, and into thoughtful dark eyes which changed the twist into desire. She looked away quickly and poured herself a glass of water.

"Yes, Amber's lovely. She wouldn't hurt anyone, she's as gentle as they come, and yet she's strong about the things she believes in."

They both looked up as Amber approached laden with food and drinks. Zane politely accepted a bowl of french fries and Rachel waited to see if he flirted with Amber, but he didn't. Neither did he watch her walk away in her tight skirt —both of which Rachel had expected. She sat back and sighed. She really *had* been spending too much time with the wrong kind of man. And their behavior around women wasn't the only difference. The men she'd been hanging out with worked in media, careers which didn't tend to attract people who could lift a piano single-handedly, which the man sitting opposite her *definitely* could do. He was different all right, and that was no bad thing, given her track record.

"My kids love her," he said.

There was that wrench in her stomach again. It was strange that this man could inflict so many contortions to her stomach in such a short space of time. Maybe different wasn't so good after all.

"So how many kids do you have?" Rachel asked, in what she hoped was only a vaguely interested voice.

"Fifteen," he said with a straight face.

"Fifteen?" She couldn't get her head around that number.

"But of course I don't bring them here all at once. That's a treat if they've done something to deserve it."

It could only mean one thing. "Like? Good marks or something?"

"Maybe. More likely a group of kids who worked well together as a team."

She grinned. "Okay, you've had your fun. You're a sports coach."

"Yeah. Rugby."

"So, it's teamwork you reward, not winning?"

"*Me mahi tahi tatou, kia manawa nui, kia toa.* The Maori rugby motto—work as one, in spirit and heart we are strong."

"That's so cool."

He leaned forward and grinned. "*And* we love to win."

She laughed. "So, you coach the local team... what else do you do around here?"

"I teach math and PE. I've seen you walk past the school. And I thought..." He paused. "That maybe you'd seen me.

Haven't you?" he asked hesitantly. "You seemed to be looking around pretty intently."

She shook her head, alarmed that she'd been seen. She'd hoped she hadn't been too obvious about what she'd been doing. "No."

He sat back in his chair and laughed. "You really know how to wound a guy."

"Why?"

"Because I'm a big macho man who likes to be noticed... especially by a beautiful woman."

The blush started in the pit of her stomach and slowly rose—there was no stopping it—until her face was glowing.

"Hey, that blush made up for it." Zane grinned and took another french fry. "Don't tell me you don't get called 'beautiful' all the time. You *must* be used to it."

Rachel shrugged. "The world in which I work calls everything 'beautiful', nothing is ever less than superlative. I guess it sounded different coming from you."

"Well, I don't know where your world is, but I only ever say things I mean."

"That makes you very unusual."

"And that makes *you* very cynical."

Rachel opened her eyes wide in surprise and lifted her cup of weak black tea, trying to hide her discomfort. She took a sip and their eyes met above her teacup. He looked concerned.

"I'm sorry," he said. "I'm sure you're not cynical. I didn't mean to imply..."

"It's okay. I just hadn't thought of myself as being cynical. But I guess you're right." She replaced the cup in the saucer. "So tell me about you. How long have you been working as a teacher in Akaroa?"

"Coming up to a year. Before that I was based in Auckland."

"But…" She frowned. "Your family is here, at Ti Tahi?"

His smile faded a little. "They are. But I moved to Auckland when I was ten." He paused. "My mother lived there. She liked the idea of me living with her."

"Like the *idea*?"

"Yeah. It didn't last. With the help of my step-father who didn't last much longer than me with Mum, I went knocking on the door of St Stephens. It's a Maori boys' boarding school. I decided pretty early on that was my best option."

"They must have been surprised."

"If they were, they didn't let on. They got in contact with my whanau and I stayed that night and then for the next seven years." He toyed with a french fry, dunking it into some ketchup and then wiping it off again, before looking up at her. "It saved my life. My mother wasn't what you'd call maternal and the only other option, where she lived, was the gangs."

"It must have been hard for you."

He shrugged. "It is what it is."

"And you returned. You don't find Akaroa small after Auckland?"

"Yes. That's why I came. I couldn't stand the city. I couldn't breathe."

She smiled. "I was the opposite. I grew up in Akaroa and felt I couldn't breathe so went to Wellington."

"Could you breathe there?"

It was a simple enough question, but not one that had been asked before. She nodded. "For a while I thought I could. But it wasn't the right sort of breathing, if you know what I mean. It just passed for breathing."

"Then you should stay away. What is it exactly you do?"

She nearly choked on her tea. He really didn't have a clue, and she decided to keep it that way. It was refreshing. He wanted to talk with her, to be with her, simply because of who she was, not *what* she was, or what she could do for him. "I'm a chef. All us sisters are foodies. My other sister Lizzi runs this great café in Tekapo, the Mackenzie country. I have a couple of commitments from my old job and then I'm free to decide what to do next. I'll see what comes up."

"Why not stay here? I take it that breathing *is* easier here?" he asked with that disarming grin.

"It's better. Definitely better. But it has its challenges. Dad, being the main one."

"I've always found your father to be pretty cool. He's on the Board of Directors at our school and he seems to be one of the good guys."

"He is. But he's getting older and refuses to deal with things. Like the garden. Like the house. He sees anything we kids offer to do, or try to do, as an insult to him, as if we're easing him into old age. We're not, but…'"

Zane slipped his hand across the table and placed it on hers. She stopped speaking and stilled instantly, glancing down at his large hand over hers. There was no pressure, no possessiveness, only a brush of comfort. She looked up into his eyes, their brown, darker now, like the best kind of dark melting chocolate, pure and delicious.

"But he doesn't see it that way," Zane finished her sentence. "It's hard because you're his kid. My father's the same. I'm forever finding him knee-deep in mud trying to rescue a lamb or something. But we have our secret weapon —my gran. She'll divert him and let us kids get on and fix things up. That way, it's all done and he keeps his *mana*, his respect. That's what your dad's scared of losing."

He withdrew his hand and Rachel felt its loss. Like a soft mohair blanket—light but warm—withdrawn on a chilly day. She shivered. Both at the loss and his words. He was right.

"How come you're so wise?"

His grin cracked open his face, like a shaft of sunlight on

his dark features. He shrugged. "Born that way, darlin'." As soon as he said it, the grin faded, as if he was concerned that he'd been too familiar.

Rachel couldn't remember the last time anyone had been worried that they'd been too familiar with her.

"I reckon you were. And I reckon your gran did a great job bringing you up in those early years."

"She'd appreciate that. She's always telling me what a fantastic *taua* she is. Trouble is, she's right."

"She sounds wonderful. I'd love to meet her." The words were out before she could censor them. They came straight from a place she hadn't spoken from for a long time. Her heart.

"Then you must come to the marae and I'll introduce you to everyone."

"That would be nice."

"*And* I'll come over and help sort your dad's garden out." He paused. "How shall I get in touch?"

She hesitated. She'd had so much bad stuff from her ex via her phone, that she was reluctant to give her new number to anyone. She pulled a napkin toward her, he passed her a pen, and she wrote the phone number of Belendroit on it. Somehow it felt right. More traditional.

"Thanks," she said. "I'd really appreciate it. As would my brothers and sisters. And even Dad will eventually. But, you must let me do something in return."

He frowned. "We've a fundraiser coming up. It would be great if you could help out."

Rachel was disappointed. She'd thought he hadn't known about her fame. But maybe he'd simply been clever in not acknowledging it. Because it sure looked like he wanted to use it.

"You don't have to, not if you're busy," he said, obviously reading her expression.

"No, you're helping *me* out, so it's only right for me to help you. It's fine, honestly. It's what I do."

"Well, if you're sure. That would be great. I'll ask the organizer to get in touch with you."

"Sure," she said with a tight smile, rising out the chair. "Look, I'd best get back." She went to pay but he rose and placed his hand more firmly this time over hers as she brought out a note from her purse.

"Please, allow me. I butted in on your afternoon with your sister."

Again, that feeling as if she'd stepped into a different world. The veil of suspicion, which had lowered at the mention of her involvement with a fundraiser, lifted. He was such a gentleman, *and* such a hunk, that instead of feeling suspicious about his motives, instead of feeling insulted that he wanted to pay, she felt wonderfully cosseted, like a treasure he'd found and wanted to protect from harm.

"Well, okay, thanks."

Outside, the town was busy with tourists enjoying the summer sunshine on the beach and on the shady verandas of cafés, overlooking the harbor.

"It's been great talking, Rachel. I'll call you later, okay?"

She nodded. It was more than okay. Again that grin before he walked away. She watched him, unable to look away. Apart from the impressive physique, he was an impressive man. Confident in himself, sure of himself and—something she hadn't thought about in relation to a man for a long time—he was kind. He turned suddenly and she was caught for a second time. She blushed and he grinned, before walking across the street and disappearing around a corner.

She was embarrassed to have been caught out—not cool, not cool at all—but the embarrassment passed. Cool was something for Wellington, not here. Cool was about appearances and it seemed Zane Black wasn't concerned at all about *them*. He took things as he found them—if he liked them, that was. And, she grinned to herself, it seemed he liked her.

For a brief moment, she wondered what her future would have been like if Zane Black had been her ex-boyfriend from Ti Tahi Bay marae; if *he'd* been the reason that she'd returned to Akaroa, the reason why she kept looking into the school-yard, trying to find a dark-haired girl of ten years of age. She wondered how different things might have been if Zane Black had been the father of her child.

2

---

*R*achel had forgotten the profusion of flowers to be found in the garden at Belendroit. In summer Belendroit was at its best with towering foxgloves, lupins, and wildflowers. Unhindered by pruning, the clematis had beaten the stranglehold of weeds to valiantly fight for space in the wild garden and had wound its way up one of the lanterns, diffusing its light at night. Leaves of the clematis tapped at the windows when a stray breeze took them, making the place feel alive. Beyond them, where the grass grew longer before disappearing into the trees, wildflowers grew—in all shades from bright orange and purple through to soft blue and white—rising on slender stalks, arching toward the sun. Rachel had been here several months now and had only in the last few days—since her afternoon with Zane—noticed the profusion of color and scent. How had she missed seeing it all before?

She lifted a bright orange wildflower that was in danger of bending too far toward the road and cupped it between her fingers, before smelling it. She grunted softly in surprise at the delicacy of such a wild thing, before resting it on a neighboring plant, and carried on walking up toward the house.

She was hot after her daily walk back from Akaroa. She'd been walking rather than taking her car for a week now, somehow managing to bump into Zane, accidentally on purpose, each time. Every day, at four in the afternoon, Zane would emerge from school as she called into the café to see Amber, or as she sat with a coffee looking out at the harbor and the summer visitors. Their conversations were always playful, fun, and increasingly flirtatious, making her feel young again somehow, even though Zane was a good four years older than her. There was something about being with him that took her out of herself, made her aware of things around her, and the sensations within her. And she couldn't get enough of those feelings—nor him.

Rachel walked past her car, dusty after a week's disuse, and up the veranda steps to where her father sat reading. He let his glasses drop on his nose and peered at her.

"Evening, Rachel. Had a good day?"

"Yes, thanks, Dad. You?"

"Same as usual. Unlike you, I suspect." He gestured toward the car. "That's the fifth day in a row you've walked into town. Not that I'm counting," he added with a smile.

"Right! And why not? The weather's been sunny—good for a walk." She sat in one of the chairs and poured herself a glass of water.

"It's good. About time you saw the world around you as something other than a view to admire from a car window. Or through a camera lens, come to that."

She settled for a vaguely reproving glare. It was the best she could do in response to his jibe. It was too nice a day to argue with her father, and *that* had nothing to do with the sun and all to do with her memories of talking with Zane, of the way his eyes looked at her, making her dizzy with desire.

She shifted her gaze to the abundance of the garden where bright red poppies rose from a carpet of pale pink thyme.

She inhaled the mingled scents. "The flowers here are amazing. I remember Mum used to have huge bowls of them all over the house."

Her father's mouth twisted but he didn't look up.

"She always used to pick them," Rachel continued. "The garden was always perfect and she kept the house so nice. *And* sorted us all out, too. I don't know how she managed it."

"I don't know how your mother managed *many* things." He sighed and set down his paper and fixed his gaze on Rachel once more. "You *can* pick them yourself, you know. The flowers I mean. Bring them into the house."

Rachel was surprised she hadn't thought of it. She shrugged. "I guess. But that was something Mum did. I'm not Mum. She was a nurturer and I'm so *obviously* not."

"How can you say that, when your career is about food. Isn't that nurturing?"

"Not in front of a studio audience, it's not. It's... *entertainment* more than anything."

"Anyway, what are you doing about those remaining programmes you're committed to? You don't seem in a rush to return to Wellington to film them."

The warm afterglow of her time with Zane immediately evaporated.

"No. I don't want to go back. Not yet."

"You have to face reality sometime," Jim said impatiently. He got up and walked into the kitchen.

For once Rachel wasn't bothered by her father's needling. She was filled with the afterglow of snippets of exchanges with Zane, of a buzz of contentment, and she wanted to hold onto it as long as possible. She followed her father inside where he was tying a cotton apron around his waist. He picked out some potatoes from a drawer and began to peel one.

"Do you want a hand?"

"I may be old, but I'm not helpless, you know."

Rachel shook her head and picked up the tea towel instead and began drying up the lunch things.

"I know you're not helpless, but that doesn't mean you can't accept a little help now and then. Especially while I'm here. You may as well make use of me."

He stilled instantly. "You know, I've had an idea. Why not have your film crew come to you?" He gestured to the sprawling old interior of the homestead. "Film your episodes here."

"Are you kidding?" was her first response.

"No. It's a genuine brainwave," he said, in all seriousness.

She looked around the kitchen through professional eyes. What was lacking in efficiency and modern appliances was made up for by the eccentricities and character of the old place. The kitchen table dominated the large space. Behind that was the butler sink in the wooden bench top and two long concertina windows, which folded back to reveal a view of the bay, framed by pohutukawa trees from which lanterns hung. At night they could be seen from Akaroa. It was a setting which her agent would jump at. Then she looked at the antiquated appliances, the rusting edges of the dishwasher, the Aga which had been installed in the 1950s.

"I can't cook on this!"

"What do you mean? You *do* cook on this. You cook *wonderfully* in this kitchen. Most of the world cooks wonderfully under these conditions. Not everyone has all the latest gadgets, you know." He huffed irritably and continued to peel the potatoes. "Trouble with you, my girl, is that you don't know what most of the world is like. *This* is real, not that stuff you cook on." He slid the pot onto the hot plate and stomped off.

Rachel lingered in the kitchen, considering her father's words as she took another look at the kitchen. He was right. Most of the world *did* cook in kitchens like this—old, familiar, battered and, she had to admit, charming. But people wanted aspirational cooking, didn't they? Her marketing brand had always been high end, glamorous cuisine, the sort of cooking which suggested a lifestyle which women of all ages and backgrounds aspired to.

She walked around the kitchen, smoothing her hand along the wooden bench tops, which had acquired the patina of long use, her duck-egg blue bowls lined up along one side. Above her a rustic wooden pot rack hung from the ceiling, dangling pots and pans mostly from her range, mingled with her mother's and grandmother's worn utensils. And then there was the Aga—worn, marked, but very, very real and full of character. She paused before the window and folded them back wide, allowing the wall behind the sink to disappear and the view of the bay to dominate the space.

Why hadn't she seen it before? This place was perfect. Maybe not her usual brand, but everyone developed and tweaked their brand, didn't they? She'd keep a tight rein on what was brought in for the shoot. Nothing to alter the image, only a few essentials to make sure the cooking itself went smoothly. Thinking about it, her new kitchen-ware range would go perfectly here—its modern lines and nod to nostalgia would fit right in with Belendroit's character. The whole would be a mixture of old and new, not competing but blending the best of both worlds. With her back to the window, she stood at the old wooden island, and looked into the room. She gripped the edges of the island and grinned. Plenty of room for the cameras in front and, providing they didn't shoot when the light was bright behind her, it would work out fine.

For once, her father had come up with a brilliant idea. She reached for the phone. The sooner she got this organized, the sooner it'd be done and she could meet her commitments and move on.

IT WAS past six and the Akaroa pub was packed. Rachel had managed to secure a window seat for her and her brother, Gabe, newly returned from working overseas. She watched him wend his way through the crowds with their drinks. He greeted people as he passed with his easy-going style. He was so deceptive, Rachel thought, as she watched him exchange pleasantries with a couple as he passed by. No one would know that, behind that incredible ease and charm, a cord of steel ran through his long, lean body. And it was this strength which made him so sought after by the international group Doctors without Borders.

"So," she asked Gabe, as he handed her a glass of wine. "How was Papua New Guinea?"

Gabe's smile faded. "It's an amazing country, but the things I saw... the violence..." He took a swig of beer. "Let's not talk about that. Tell me about filming. Dad said you're going to go ahead and film at Belendroit."

"Yes. It's all arranged. My agent was so relieved to get the episodes completed that she's organized everything for next week."

"Brilliant suggestion of Dad's. I'm glad you took it up."

"Me too. I don't know why I didn't think of it before."

"I reckon living here suits you," said Gabe. "I've never seen you so relaxed."

Rachel glanced away, trying to hide a smile which seemed

to be permanently on her lips at the moment. She shrugged. "It's summer, a break from work, what's not to be relaxed about?"

"Exactly. But you've always been fidgety with no work before."

She couldn't argue with that. "Maybe I'm just becoming more chilled as I get older."

Gabe scoffed. "Doubt that. Not without some encouragement. And some of my patients are suggesting you're receiving exactly that."

She frowned. Simply the hint of gossip rattled her, bringing back images of indiscreet social media posts, of conjecture about her love life.

"Not like that," said Gabe, obviously able to read her like a book. "They're simply saying that you've been seen in company—regular company—one man in particular."

"Oh, well, that's true, I guess." She could hardly deny it. A day hadn't gone by of the past few weeks without Zane making an appearance wherever she was. "Akaroa is a small town."

"Big enough to avoid someone if you wanted to. And also to see someone if you wanted to." He paused. "Do you like him? I don't want you messing him around. He's a good bloke."

"Of course I like him. He's..." She fizzled out as she wondered how to describe him. "He's a gentleman. He's really nice." Rachel could see different thoughts flitting through Gabe's brain as he raised an eyebrow and grinned. "Gabe," she warned.

"That's good! That's all I'm thinking. Honest" He grinned again, picked up the menu and looked around for the waitress.

"I'm helping him out with the school fundraiser. I'm going to use some of the equipment at the school for a cookery demonstration. Apparently the ticket sales are going really well."

"That's great. I bet Zane's chuffed."

"He doesn't know," she said quickly. "He'll be away for the week before the fundraiser so he won't see any of the advertising and so I thought I'd keep it a surprise." It would also mean she could enjoy his treating her like a regular girl for a little while longer. But she didn't share this with Gabe. "You won't tell him, will you?"

"No, not if you don't want me to. Of course not."

"Cool." She sat back and took a sip of her chilled white wine.

"Anyway," he said with a grin. "It appears you're irresistible."

Rachel looked up with a start into Zane's dark eyes. His face broke into a grin, radiating lines from his mouth and eyes like the sun emerging from a dark, serious-looking cloud.

"Zane!" She glanced at Gabe, embarrassed by her schoolgirl tone.

"Rachel, Gabe," acknowledged Zane. "I was passing and saw you through the window. Mind if I join you?"

"Zane, mate!" Gabe rose from his chair. "You don't need to ask. I'll get you a beer, and"—he glanced from Zane to Rachel and back again—"and I'll leave you in my sister's capable hands."

Rachel would have hit him if he were closer but he'd risen from his chair and was on his way to the bar, as if he'd anticipated her reaction.

"How are you?" asked Zane as he sat opposite and gazed at her appreciatively. Rachel could take any amount of that. "You're looking… good."

She grinned at his low-key compliment. She was so used to men making her extravagant compliments, whether she warranted them or not. "Excellent. Because I'm *feeling* good." She hesitated. "Especially now you're here." She indicated Gabe who was leaning against the bar, chatting amiably with one of the waitresses. "Little brothers tease so much."

Zane glanced at Gabe. "It's our sworn duty. To make sure sisters and nieces and cousins don't get too big for their boots."

"Are you like that with your family?"

"Yep. I give them all a hard time."

"Well, thank goodness for men who aren't related to me."

"I can tell you, in all sincerity, that I'm very pleased to be a member of that group."

His grin made her blush.

"Zane Black!" said Gabe, placing a beer in front of his friend. "You've done the impossible! You've made my sister blush."

Zane gave Rachel a very self-satisfied smile. "Is that right?"

Rachel cleared her throat and shot Gabe a warning look. "It's hot in here, that's all."

"Not as hot as you're going to be in that kitchen of yours soon."

"Oh," said Zane, frowning in confusion. "Are you having a party or something?"

"No, it's—"

Rachel kicked Gabe under the table. "It's nothing." She really didn't want Zane to know about her work. Not yet. It seems no one had told him and he was totally unaware of her TV show. He might be friends with Gabe but Gabe was so unimpressed with celebrity that he probably wouldn't have even thought to tell his friend what Rachel did for a living. "I'm cooking dinner for Dad and Gabe later. You know, the usual."

Gabe rolled his eyes at Rachel and struck up a conversation with a friend at a neighboring table.

"Ah," said Zane. "Lucky them."

"You'll have to come round some time."

"Sounds good."

"How about after the fundraiser?"

"Cool. I'll be back from Christchurch that morning. Hope it goes okay. The teams need the money."

"Oh, I think you can confidently expect it will."

"How? I've been out of the loop with other commitments."

"I hear numbers have exceeded expectations with the arrival of some last-minute acts."

"Really? That's fantastic. It'll mean that anything above the target can go towards another group."

"But they won't have to do any more fundraising, will they? I mean, all those car-washing sessions and sausage sizzles, you can forget them if you've made enough money from the weekend, surely?"

"No way. Those kids have to work for what they want. Simply because we've done well at this fundraiser doesn't mean they can slacken off. They need to learn they have to work hard to get on in the world. I'm not having them waste time on Xbox, or Facebook, or whatever the latest fashion is."

She laughed. "You're not into any of that, are you?" She knew the answer and loved the fact he wasn't.

"No. I know enough about social media to not want anything to do with it."

"I know what you mean. How my brother Max, and his wife Laura, cope with it all is beyond me. Mind you, Max would do anything for Laura, he's besotted with her."

"Ah well. Love makes fools of us all."

There was a sudden silence in which Gabe turned back to them. "Any more drinks, anyone?"

"Nah," said Zane. "I need to be going."

Rachel rose. "Me, too. Thanks Gabe. I'll call you later."

Zane opened the door for Rachel and she stepped out into the warm evening. "Are you walking?" asked Zane.

"Yes." She stood twisting her bag in her hands like a school girl, hoping he wasn't going to disappear immediately.

"Good. Because I am, too."

They fell into step and were soon at Beach Road.

"What you said back there, about love making fools of us all."

"What about it?"

"You called me cynical when we first met. I reckon *you're* the cynical one."

"Once bitten, twice shy."

"Want to tell me about it?"

"Not really." He looked at her askance as they walked along the harbor side. "But I guess you're not going to rest until I do."

"You've got it." They'd reached a picnic bench under the trees.

"Well then. Take a seat, and I'll tell you."

"I thought you had to be somewhere."

"I did. Alone with you."

There was that look again in his eyes which transformed her into a fluttering melting mess of a woman. It was a wonderful feeling. She sat on the picnic bench, her feet nearly touching his as he sat opposite her. It was all she could do not to not move her foot until it touched his. She was wearing jandals, he, smart dress shoes. She shifted her foot and brushed her big toe against the polished leather of his foot so gently she didn't think he'd notice. It did strange things to her inside.

He didn't take his eyes off her but his smile broadened a little. "Okay. What do you want to know?"

Rachel kept her foot where it was, needing that connection now. "You said once bitten, twice shy. I can't imagine anyone biting you. Not without them coming off worse, anyway."

His gaze was level. "I can take a nip or two without retaliating. You can try it some time, if you like."

The blatant sexual innuendo made the heat rise even higher. She was thankful for the cooling breeze blowing in from the harbor. She licked her lips as her gaze lowered to his and tried to regain focus. "Maybe later." She shifted her foot closer to his so that he'd definitely notice. "In the meantime, I'd be interested to know why you're avoiding love. What happened?"

"*That*, Rachel, is a very personal question."

"It is," she admitted. "But I'm helluva interested in the reply."

He grinned. "There's no huge mystery. I fell in love, we were engaged to be married. I thought the world of her and thought she did of me. But..." He paused as his eyes wandered back into a world of his past. "But then I fell in a game. My knee was bust and so, apparently, was my relationship. You see, it appeared she was keener on the glamor of being an All Black's girlfriend, than *my* girlfriend."

"Oh, I'm sorry. But maybe you're better off without her if she's like that."

"Yeah. But it didn't feel like that at the time. I guess that only really hit home when, a month later, she started a relationship with one of my mates who's still an All Black with his sights on management. She got what she wanted."

"And your friend? He doesn't think he's being used?"

"He doesn't care. He's using her as much as she's using him. A perfect exchange. Ah, that's me being cynical again. You're right. Maybe cynicism comes with age."

"Are you calling me old?" she teased.

"No. I'm calling you... experienced. Something's happened to make you want to change your life. You haven't told me much about your work in Wellington except that you're a chef. I guess the long hours got too much. It must be hard to have relationships with people when you work unsociable hours."

She half-laughed. Her work hours had only occasionally extended into the evening. It was on the tip of her tongue to tell him but she stopped herself. His ignorance of her fame was refreshing. Besides, he'd find out soon enough. At the weekend, in fact. And wouldn't he get a surprise? Especially about the fundraising.

"I seem to attract the wrong person. I've no idea why."

He sat forward. "*I* know why."

She looked up surprised. "Why?"

"Because you don't think enough of yourself."

"I don't?"

"No. I've seen you automatically apologize when someone bumps into you. I've seen you instinctively give something to someone when you could have used it yourself. And I bet you're the same way with men. Too giving, not thinking about yourself enough."

She swept her hand away, embarrassed that he'd noticed so much about her. "That's as may be. But that's not all of me. There are other aspects which might surprise you." She thought of how she could switch on the inner diva once the lights were on, and she was on familiar ground with her cooking.

He took hold of her hand. "Really? I'm not sure I like surprises. Maybe you could begin by showing me now?" He raised a suggestive brow.

The sensuous way he stroked her hand made her want to show him anything and everything. "Well, I'm not beyond taking things which are offered to me." She smiled sweetly and received the hoped-for response.

He brushed his lips across her knuckles and looked over her hand into her eyes. "How about if I offer you a kiss?"

"Then I'd take it."

He leaned closer and swept his lips against hers. He swallowed and sat back, his eyes dark with arousal, but she noticed he'd dropped her hand.

"So you take a kiss. What else is there to know about you that I haven't already pieced together?"

"I'm like my father in that I'm a bit of a closet diva."

"Really? I *am* surprised. I didn't imagine that."

She shrugged. "By day a diligent cook, by night an overacting showgirl."

"You know, that sounds more attractive than I first imagined. What kind of showgirl?"

"If you're imagining pole dancing, you're entirely off the mark."

"That's a shame. My mind wandered for a minute there."

She grinned and rose. He shot out his hand and tugged her to him and she fell, laughing, onto his lap. He slipped his arms around her. "I've been waiting all week for this."

"Me too."

There was a moment when all they could hear was the ripple of the quiet tide coming into the bay before their lips came together. For such a big man, used to control, his lips were gentle, curious even, as if they were exploring not only her mouth, but her mind and body, assessing, piecing her together. But when her tongue touched his lips, any tentativeness vanished and he met her tongue with a sensuousness and manliness which made her gasp. She was instantly aroused, like she'd never been before.

She shifted on his lap to give her better access to his mouth, which she explored as he did, with tender lips, a probing tongue, and nips and nibbles which sent her crazy with desire. She held his head steady between her hands, not wanting him to move an inch, demanding access to him.

"Um," he said as they parted. "You *are* demanding. I hadn't imagined that either."

She shook her head, suddenly shy. "I'm not usually. But…I just can't seem to get enough of you."

Suddenly the sound of someone coming around the corner made her jump up. "I'd better go." She shrugged. "Dad will be wondering where I am."

"Like a teenager, all over again." He smiled.

She shook her head. "Not really." Her teenage experience was very different from most people's.

"Your Dad never wondered where you were? Lucky you."

"No. Not so lucky."

"Sounds like you've a story to tell. Maybe you'll tell it to me some time."

"Maybe."

"I'll see you around."

She nodded and walked back to Belendroit. As she entered the garden she looked back to the place where they'd kissed and she touched her lips, reliving his kiss and imagining the next time they'd meet… and hoping they'd be alone.

She was about to emerge onto the sunlit lawn when, instead, she gave way to an impulse and walked through the woods, gathering the flowers. She only stopped when she couldn't carry anymore. With arms full of fragrant, delicate flowers of every hue, she walked back to the house, wondering where her mother had kept all the vases.

3

"I hear you're seeing Zane Black," said Jim Connelly, before taking a sip of his morning coffee and shaking out his newspaper.

Rachel nearly choked on her coffee. "I'm... having coffee with him from time to time. He's a nice guy. Any objections?"

"He's a good man. My only objection would be if you were trying to use him for some other purpose."

Rachel stilled. She forced herself to replace her cup onto the saucer carefully and sit back, brushing a piece of flaky croissant pastry from her jeans. She looked up into his direct gaze, crowned by a pair of fierce white eyebrows. She looked around for something to divert his attention. But even the two mad cocker spaniels, Stanley and Boo, lay asleep on the sunny veranda for once, providing no distraction. "I don't know what you mean."

"Yes, you do. I'm referring to the *real* reason you're here, at Belendroit."

"Oh! Maybe you'll tell me what that is, then."

"If you wish. You're here for one reason only—you've come here to try to track down your child."

His last word hung between them like a threat and a promise, and couldn't be unsaid.

Rachel's mouth dried. "I…" She jumped up and walked to the edge of the veranda, and looked out across the bay, a deceptive gray sheet of satin under a bright silver sky. The heat of the morning was contained under the spreading clouds. It would rain later.

The cane of her father's chair squeaked as he got up. She felt his hand on her shoulder. She didn't move, not even when he squeezed her shoulder and whispered her pet name. "Rach, come on. I understand. I've been waiting for you to do something like this for years. Your mother always thought you would."

Her shoulders slumped then, his words draining the fight out of her. She twisted around and looked into eyes which held nothing but sympathy now. "You didn't say anything."

"I was following orders. Your mother's. You know, it was a beautiful day when you told your mother and me. Although I think she already knew."

She licked her lips. "But… I hadn't told her."

"No. She knew these things though. She saw the changes in you. I'd been blind up till then."

"You were busy."

"Yep." He sighed ruefully. "Too busy to notice many things. Besides, I hadn't even thought of you as an adult. And there you suddenly were, a grown-up woman and I was devastated. My little girl. Pregnant, at sixteen years of age."

"I didn't feel little. I felt grown up with the world at my feet. I felt invincible."

"I always imagined the boy must have taken advantage of you."

"No. It was probably the other way around. No one took advantage of me. I took control then and I intend to take control now. Dad…" She tried to hold back the tears which pricked at the back of her eyes. "I can't go on without doing something... making some kind of contact, reparation, whatever." She shook her head, trying to contain the pain. "I brought a beautiful baby girl into the world and gave her away." She turned to her father. "What kind of person would do such a thing?"

"A very *young* person. It wasn't cruel or mean or uncaring, it was kind. Your mother couldn't take the child on, because she didn't know how long she had to live. She knew she'd soon be too sick to take care of her own children, let alone grandchildren. She made the best decision she could. Neither you, nor she, were in a position to care for the child. So putting her up for adoption was the only choice."

Rachel looked out at the still bright bay, the sunlight somehow focused and heightened as it passed through the thin layer of cloud and bounced off the water. Her eyes watered slightly and she pulled down her sunglasses from on top of her head. She could still remember her dark-haired daughter's baby smell. Just the memory of the smell of her child, snuggled against her for those brief moments before she'd been taken away, took Rachel back to the place of her deepest sadness. Seemed you could forget many things but not the smell of your newborn child. "I wish I hadn't done it. I should have looked after her. But it's not too late."

"Not too late? Of course it is. Goodness knows where she is." He frowned, deep in thought. "We could probably find out if she's okay, discover a little about her, but there's no way her family want a connection. They took her on that condition. And it's not fair on Zane to try to find her through him. From what I've heard he likes you, *really* likes you."

"I'm not!" But even as she spoke she questioned her motives. She really, really liked Zane, too. But wasn't there a small part of her which thought he could help her? "Dad, I've been thinking of nothing but *her*. It drives me crazy not knowing what she looks like. Have you really no idea as to her identity? You know her age, the color of her hair. There must be other things you know."

He shook his head. "No, I know as much as you. I don't even know if she's living on the marae with Mrs Tau's whanau or with another branch of the family, elsewhere in New Zealand, or out of it, come to that."

"But there can't be that many kids around who fit the description."

"You want to bet? A girl. Brown hair, brown eyes. There are always kids coming and going. I have no idea which one is your daughter, and I haven't tried to find out. You have to forget her, Rach."

"I tried to, to begin with at least. But I can't anymore. My life in Wellington is a mess—"

"Those photos?"

"*Yes*, those photos. What does it come to when you can't trust someone with a photograph?"

"He was a slimeball, Rachel. And I don't know why you couldn't recognize it."

"Yes, obviously a lack on my part," she said facetiously. Why did her father always have to make her responsible for all the crap things which happened to her?

"What about your work? That used to mean so much to you."

"I can't seem to find any joy in it anymore. All I can think about is my daughter."

"But she's not *yours*, darling. Don't you understand? Your mother and I made the arrangements with Mrs Tau and her tribe, and we all agreed that it was best for the child to be raised in their extended family, without contact from you, or any of us. The father only stayed around long enough to get into trouble before he disappeared overseas. So there's no guarantee the child is still here either."

"Wherever she is, I just want to know she's okay, hopefully see her." She shrugged. "I don't know, Dad, it's like a gaping hole in my life which I need to fill—at least a bit—before I can think of doing anything else. It's not as if I can talk about it to any of the others."

"We thought it best for no one to know. Best for you to be in Wellington with your mother when you began to show."

"Keep it quiet," she said bitterly.

He shook his head. "Maybe we did the wrong thing, but you were so young. We only wanted to protect you, to give you the future that our bright daughter deserved."

She shifted away from his embrace. "It's okay. It's done." She'd thought over her parents' decisions so many times, decisions which had influenced her own, and wondered what her life would have been like if she'd kept her baby. For years the answer had been that it had been the right decision, that she'd got the life she'd always dreamed about. But now? Now, she wasn't so sure.

"And can't be undone," said her father. "And you know what that means. Mrs Tau and her family are your daughter's guardians and you're not a part of her life. And that's the way she wants it to stay."

She looked up suddenly. "But any arrangements like that fall outside the New Zealand adoption law. I've looked into it, Dad."

"You surely don't intend to take her away from the world she's grown up in? Tell me you don't mean to do that."

"Of course I don't. I don't want to do anything that could be detrimental to her. But what if she's asked about me? What if she's curious?"

"Then no doubt we would have heard."

"How can you be so sure?"

"I can't, of course I can't. But this is all crazy, Rachel. Leave it alone."

"I can't. Are you still in touch with Mrs Tau?"

"I see her all the time but I can't say we're particularly friendly, not after what happened. And nothing will have changed. She won't welcome your interference, and nor will the tribe. They are very protective of their people; there's been too long a history of interference into their lives and they're determined to look after their own."

"But I'm not here to interfere. Just to see her. Just to…"

"You don't know what you want, do you?"

"I know something needs to change, to heal, or something, before I can get on with my life."

"Rachel! You're *not* wanted. If you were, Mrs Tau would have contacted me. She didn't. You *have* to leave it. Move on with your life."

"It's too late for that."

Her father's expression changed instantly. The shaggy white brows lowered and his blue eyes became icy blue. "What do you mean?"

Even at twenty-six years of age, Rachel felt the familiar nerves at the sudden change. "I mean that I've decided to do things properly. I've already written to the tribal authority seeking permission to find out my daughter's name, her whereabouts, and to meet with her."

Jim Connelly pulled himself up to his full, not insignificant, height, his face aghast. "You've done *what*?"

"I've done what I should have done years ago. And if they won't help me then I'll employ a lawyer to look into my access rights under the Guardianship Act. You can't stop me, Dad."

He closed his eyes. "No. All I can do is be here for you, to pick up the pieces. It's not going to happen, Rachel, and the sooner you get your head around that, the happier you'll be."

Rachel shook her head. "You're wrong. I won't be happy until I find her." She stepped away, wishing with all her heart that she could be the woman her father thought she was, that she could walk away from her child and step into a future of riches and fame. But she'd tried that and it hadn't worked. And she knew, with all her heart, that she couldn't move on without at least trying to find her child.

THE NEXT DAY Rachel returned from Amber's café downhearted. As usual she'd timed her daily walk into town to coincide with either a school break or end of school. She'd paused, ostensibly window shopping, watching the reflection in the window of the kids pouring out of the school gates. But today she didn't have the courage to turn around and search individual faces as she'd done in the past. Instead, she watched them run out onto the street and into the adjacent park as one, like a tide of children, laughing and full of life. One of them was hers, she just knew it. But she hadn't the first clue which one. And, if her father was right, she didn't stand a chance.

She paused by the café, but wasn't in the mood for chatting to Amber. She continued on to the water front and let the cooling breeze calm her thoughts. What if the tribal board refused her request, as her father believed? What then?

There'd be no point in hanging around if they did. She may as well take the lucrative US contract her agent was keen for her to accept. The offer wouldn't be around forever. She might have escaped her crazy love life by running home but that was all she'd done. Nothing else was solved—not her fears that she'd never find a man who wanted her, only for herself, and not for what she could bring them, and not her fears that she'd given a part of herself away that she'd never get back. Her child.

On impulse, she bought a bottle of wine and slung it in

her bag and began the long walk back to the Connelly home-stead. She'd sit out on the jetty tonight, with only the lights from the lanterns for company. She'd drink the wine and try to forget her heartache. She'd have the place to herself. Her father was at a rehearsal of his local amateur dramatics society and she relished the idea of a peaceful evening, without the threat of confrontation, without the occasional disapproving glance.

But, as Belendroit came into view around the headland, her heart sank. The sound of wood being chopped greeted her. Seemed like her father had had a change of plans. Then she frowned. Her father and the ax weren't closely acquainted. Chopping wood was one of the few jobs he allowed his sons to do for him. Out of her four brothers, Rob and Cameron lived away, so the task usually fell to Gabe, as the son who lived closest, or to Max on one of his visits during which he used to let off steam by chopping firewood. But it seemed, since his marriage, Max had little steam to let off anymore. And neither Gabe nor Max were expected today.

She walked around the back of the house and peered around the leafy wisteria vine which was the main means of support of the outer corner of the veranda. What she saw made her inhale sharply. Zane Black's bare arms were extended above his head, the muscles gleaming under the hot sun as they fell down onto the thick wide stump which he was splitting. The ax fell with a sharp thump which reverberated on the hard, dry ground, at the same time the wood split, sending kindling every which way. But Rachel wasn't looking at the kindling. She couldn't take her eyes off his naked arms, chest and stomach, which displayed the kind of six-pack only seen on professional athletes, even, apparently, those who were no longer professional.

She clenched her hands in a vain attempt to control the

visceral response she had to his beauty and strength. God help her, she wanted to walk over to him and press her nose to his chest and inhale him, lick him, do any number of things which had never occurred to her to do before. Was she going mad? It was certainly hot. She swayed a little and caught the wisteria which jerked beneath her grip. Zane looked up suddenly.

He buried the ax in the wood and stood up straight. The sight was even more arresting. "Rachel!"

That man, that body, with her name on his lips.

"Zane!" Her voice was croaky and she cleared her throat. "Zane!" she called, more decisively, and walked over to him. "I didn't expect to see you here." Particularly only partially clothed, she thought as she tried to restrain her gaze from wandering all over his glorious body.

He grinned as if he could read her mind and stepped toward her. "I'm away tomorrow so thought I'd make a start on the firewood."

"Good idea," she said, maybe too appreciatively. She tried to focus. "Thanks for doing all of this. I've been worried that tree would fall down on the house in winter but Dad wouldn't let the boys touch it."

"I guess me not being his son made it easier for him to agree. No threat, different approach. There are different ways to go about something, and it's not always so easy when there's a relationship at stake."

"I guess you're right."

He glanced at the pile of wood. "I'm just about finished. It didn't take long to get it down. Pretty rotten, but it'll make good firewood."

He stepped toward her again and she stepped away, afraid of what she'd do if she came too close to him. "Would you like a drink? Something long and cool?" she asked.

"That would be great. I'll tidy up here and then come up to the house."

"I'll have a drink waiting on the dock. It's coolest there this time of day." She walked up the steps of the house, willing the heat to leave her cheeks. She kept checking on him through the window while she changed into her bikini and sarong, before preparing a tray of snacks and drinks. Once done she continued to watch him, this time looking at his attitude, his face, so focused on what he was doing. He was full of intention and deliberate in his movements. It fitted with her first impressions of him.

He finished up and she backed away from the window. She grabbed the tray and walked outside and across the short lawn to the sandy bay and the dock that projected into the water. It was high tide and the water lapped around, sending cooling air up from below the slatted wood.

She was acutely aware of the sound of his movements as he walked from the front of the property around the back, toward the dock. She could have sworn she felt his eyes on her as she set down the tray, sat on a cushion and leaned against one of the wooden jetty piles.

She held up a glass of water and a beer as he approached. "I wasn't sure which you'd like."

"Both." He grinned. He downed the water in one and took the beer from her and sat opposite. She wished he'd sat beside her, because stopping her gaze from drifting to his shoulders and chest was hard work.

"So what have you been up to today?" he asked.

She thought briefly of the conversation she'd had with her father, of the lack of success looking at the school, and was sick of it all. "Wasting time."

He raised his eyebrow. "You know how the saying goes… you'll never get it back."

"Yeah. I know. And it's right. I bet *you* don't waste time."

"No. I've too much to do. But maybe you have, too. Sometimes people need time to think."

"I've done too much thinking and not enough acting."

He looked at her thoughtfully. "You sound different. Had a rough day?"

"You could say that." She took a sip of the wine she'd bought and sighed. "I've been trying to do the impossible, Zane, and I'm rapidly coming to the conclusion that I should restrict myself to the possible. It's a whole lot simpler, not to say more successful."

"And so what's possible for you at the moment?"

She shrugged and held up the glass of wine. "Enjoying a glass of wine in the sun in good company," she said evasively.

He smiled, satisfied, and took a swig of his beer. "I'm good company, eh?"

"Sure are."

"Good. Because so are you."

She took another sip of wine and felt a welcome lightness drift over her. "Really? All I've done is talk you into some hard labour on our land. Not sure that's so good. Not for you, at least."

He shrugged. "I don't mind. It's better than working out in a sweaty gym and besides..."

He didn't finish the sentence and she looked up at him. "Besides?"

"The sight of you in your swimming togs sure beats the sight of... well just about anything else I can think of." He grinned, narrowed his gaze out to the gray-blue hills on the opposite side of the wide harbor, and took a swig of beer.

She tried to hide her blush by looking down at her feet which nervously toyed with her jandals, as her hair fell like curtains over her face. She cleared her throat. "Swimming togs? It's a Stella McCartney bikini, I'll have you know."

"Um." He glanced quickly at her and then straight back out to the horizon. "That mesh bit at the top is nice."

It was also see-through, to the tops of her breasts anyway. This time Rachel knew that no amount of waiting would cool her down.

She jumped up. "I'm going for a swim."

She jumped off the dock and swam out across the calm water. There was a splash and the sound of strong arms slicing through the water as Zane wasted no time in following her. She continued until she was out of her depth. The water was cooler here, much cooler, and she lifted her bottom and dived down, her fingers brushing along the sandy floor. When she surfaced she found Zane directly in front of her. Her legs faltered and she dropped in the water. In an instant he reached out for her and held her. He wasn't out of *his* depth.

"Hey, I *can* swim."

"You appeared to be sinking then."

"That's only because you distracted me."

"Um, maybe I should distract you some more." Before she could answer, or maybe her lips which opened immediately were answer enough, he'd brought her towards him and she drifted through the water, and bumped against his body. His large hands slipped around her waist and she thought he was going to kiss her. But then his grip tightened, his lips quirked at the corners and he lifted her up and threw her up into the air. She landed with a yelp and a splash on her back. Allowing herself to sink down to the bottom, she swam a few long strokes under water. She could see through the water that the disturbed sand had hidden her progress. Quickly she hooked both hands around his ankle and pulled. If he hadn't been twisted around, checking to see where she'd gone, he'd have stayed put. As it was, he fell down to the bottom and reached out to grab her. She

48

pushed off and swam strongly back to shore, with Zane hard on her heels.

He thrust his fingers through his short hair as he waded toward her on the shore. "No one's got the better of me swimming since I was a kid."

Laughing, she reached for her towel. "You forget I was raised here, as much at home in the water as out of it. I know this shoreline like the back of my hand."

He reached out and took her hand and pretended to scrutinize it. "Not such a big hand, it would be easy to know." He dropped it again.

"You reckon?" She squinted up at him, the sunlight directly behind, obscuring his expression.

"Yeah, I reckon."

She couldn't help it. The challenge was there in his eyes, in his voice, and all she wanted to do was meet it. She bridged the space between them in an instant. He stilled, his lids lowered as they looked down at her with an impenetrable gaze. Whatever its meaning, it had only one effect on her and *that* her mind had no chance of controlling.

She pressed her hand against his chest, hot and wet against her soft palm. It rose as he inhaled sharply.

"Rachel," he said, his voice low with warning.

She cocked an eyebrow. "Zane?" She'd intended something light and innocent, but it emerged husky and full of promise. She swallowed and smoothed her hand upward across his chest, feeling each movement across the springy hairs and the contoured muscles acutely. Suddenly he clamped his hand over hers and she looked away from his chest, up into his eyes.

"Rachel," he growled again. "What are you doing?"

"I'd have thought that was obvious. Touching you."

"Why?"

She shrugged and grinned. "Maybe... to seduce you?"

He pulled her hand away from him, his fingers thrusting between hers before gripping it firmly. "You want to seduce me, here, now? You want me to throw you to the ground and ravish you? Hey? Is that your idea?" His tone was gruff and disapproving.

"You say that like it's a bad idea."

"That's because it is." He shifted her hand so he held it tight between both of his. "I don't *do* casual. Not anymore. I want to get to know you"—he smoothed his finger over the back of her hand—"*and* your hand, *much* better before we go any further."

"Oh." The word had no capacity to convey both how disappointed and yet how thrilled she was at the same time.

"I'm going now. I'll be away for the rest of the week but I'll see you Saturday at the fundraiser, yes?" He took her hand, glanced at it and kissed it, his lips grazing her still wet skin.

"Yes. Definitely, yes," she breathed.

He grinned and walked away, picking up his shirt as he did so. She followed him slowly up to the house which he by-passed, walking up to the drive and out onto the road beyond. He'd take the short-cut over the hills to the marae. She stood and watched him. He turned only once and gave her a brief wave.

Oh boy, she was smitten. Even more so by his control and ability to hold off where she'd have dived straight in. This man had control. This man had the ability to disarm her like no other.

RACHEL HAD FORGOTTEN how much she enjoyed her business. The school had worked hard on setting up the stage to make it look identical to Rachel's usual TV set, complete with accessories and a backdrop of the Wellington skyline, and the place was packed with locals and people from as far as Christchurch, come to see New Zealand's premier TV chef in action.

All Rachel could see was a sea of faces and she flicked her hair as she usually did with her trademark flirtation and began the show. Her inner diva had made a quick appearance and she was soon going full steam ahead, with the chat, the jokes and above all the food. This was what she knew; this was what she was good at. Soon people were literally eating out of the palm of her hand, laughter and good spirits filled the air and, from the look of the organizers' huge smiles, the money was flowing in. Rachel cast another quick look around. She'd have seen Zane if he were there, being taller than everyone else, but he wasn't. She felt disappointed. Maybe something had kept him. He'd come later, she reassured herself. She hadn't imagined any of the desire she'd seen and heard in him. He'd be there, he'd said he would. But part of her wanted him to see her in action, doing what she was good at. Part of her, a whole big part, wanted to impress him.

HE SHOULD HAVE WALKED to the school, Zane told himself, as he tried once more to find a car park. It was never this busy. There were cars everywhere—parked illegally, parked all the way down the road and around the corners onto the main street. In the end he parked at a mate's house and had to walk the half hour back to school.

He walked quickly. He was looking forward to seeing Rachel. His evening with her had changed things for him. She was totally gorgeous but she also had a vulnerability and softness which appealed strongly to him. Not to mention the sweetness. He'd told her that Amber was sweet. What he hadn't told her was that he thought she was, too. It had taken all his willpower to return straight home from her house the last time he'd seen her.

The only contact he'd had with the school during his week away had been from one of the organizers of the fundraiser, thanking him for getting Rachel involved, and the great news about the bookings for some show or other. He didn't know what. So he had no idea that the fundraiser would be so popular. Whatever Rachel was cooking for the stalls was obviously going down well.

He looked around the stalls and games in the school grounds, and frowned. For all the cars, there didn't seem to be many people in the playground or fields. Only some kids playing ball and a few people talking. They glanced across at him and greeted him as he walked by. He paused on the steps to the hall and looked around. Where was everyone? And then he heard cheers and laughter coming from inside the hall, and a voice coming from a microphone, loud and clear —Rachel's voice.

A prickle of surprise ran through him. He didn't like surprises. He liked to control his environment, he liked to understand his family and friends and be able to anticipate their moves. It was instinctive but also something honed on the rugby field under the pressure of high-profile games. And this he neither expected, nor liked. He walked slowly up the steps, unsure what he'd see inside the hall.

He stood at the back, in the shadow of a pillar, and followed the eyes of everyone else in the crowded room, to the stage where someone who looked like Rachel, someone who spoke in Rachel's voice, commanded the stage. It was her, but it wasn't her. She held herself differently, she spoke in a different way, she interacted with people differently. Instead of the self-possessed but wary person he knew, he was looking at someone flirtatious and, he had to admit, fun.

As he listened to her cooking instructions, combined with banter with the audience, and personal observations, he felt unsettled by this very public display of her charm.

"She's great, isn't she?" asked one of his nieces who had come bounding up to him. "I didn't know you knew her."

"Do *you* know her?"

She rolled her eyes. "Of course I do. Everyone knows her. She's on TV every Saturday with her cookery programme."

"What?"

His niece looked pityingly at her uncle. "You'd know that, Uncle Zane, if you ever watched TV."

He leaned his head back with a clunk against the pillar.

"And she's in—or used to be in—all the celebrity magazines. But, come to think of it, I haven't seen any Instagram posts about her for a few months… or even longer. Not since that stupid ex posted some photos of her on Facebook."

"Photos… Facebook," said Zane faintly.

"Yeah. Nude apparently. Not that many people saw them. They were taken down pretty damn smart. But I guess they're still around if you want to find them." She looked up at Zane. "Don't tell me you want to find them, Zane?"

"No, I do not!" he replied indignantly.

She grinned and raised an eyebrow. "Maybe you don't need to."

"What do you mean by that?"

"You know what I mean." She laughed and jumped out the way before teasing her uncle became a physical sport.

But Zane wasn't in the mood for reprimanding his niece. All he could think about as he stared at the stranger on the stage, was that the woman he'd thought he was coming to know had now appeared in public and revealed herself to be a completely different person—a *public* person. One who lived her life in the gossip columns and women's magazines. Someone a million miles from the person he thought he knew, from the person he wanted. He backed away. He'd left that life behind him after his fiancée had dumped him. He'd left that life behind him after he'd turned his back on the job as sports coach and commentator. It wasn't what he wanted. He wanted *real*. And the woman performing on the stage now was the opposite of that.

He looked away as Rachel's glance caught his own and walked down the steps and out into the bright sunshine of the playground. A few of the kids from his extended family were kicking a ball around the playing field and an uncle sat on a bench talking to a friend. He looked around the hills and out toward the water. This was his home. These were his people. *That*, in *there*, was nothing to do with him.

4

Zane was half way toward the school gate before he stopped himself. What was he doing? Okay, so the woman he was becoming obsessed with had turned out different to what he'd imagined. It wasn't like *that* hadn't happened before.

He looked around. People were beginning to emerge from the hall, smiles on their faces. It didn't look like *they* regretted paying for their ticket—however much that was. He plucked a programme from a nearby bench and read it through. He'd provided the rough draft but hadn't seen it in its final form. Completely different from his draft, the front page was now plastered with Rachel's professional photograph, in a kitchen setting and marked 'as seen on TV'. Then his gaze dropped to the admission price and he let out a low whistle. A quick calculation made him realize that the fundraiser had been an outstanding success.

"Zane!" He looked up to see the school principal, Ian, beckoning him over. He was talking to Rachel who kept glancing at Zane with a nervous smile.

Zane had no option but to approach Ian. Not because he

was his boss, but because of the look in Rachel's eyes. But no amount of confusion could make him reassure her.

"Rachel." He greeted her coolly.

"Zane." Her smile wilted.

Ian clapped Zane on the back. "I want to thank you for persuading Rachel to help out here. She was fantastic. Everyone loved her. And the money has come rolling in. No more fundraising required, Zane, for this trip, nor the next. That must be music to your ears."

Zane felt none of Ian's joy, only a steely determination not to change his plans. He had no intention of letting this publicity circus affect his kids. "We'll continue fundraising. It's as much for the kids as for the money."

Ian frowned. They'd never had an easy relationship. Zane's position in the community and on his tribal council meant that he was used to authority and struggled with the fact that Ian had ultimate control of the school. Luckily Ian usually agreed with Zane. But not, apparently, in this case.

"There's no point making the children work for nothing, Zane, not when Rachel has made that unnecessary." He turned to Rachel. "Thank you so much again, Rachel, for taking time out of your busy schedule to do this for us."

Rachel glanced at Zane. "I'm not so busy at the moment. I've been staying with my father for a while."

"So what's next for you?"

She glanced awkwardly at Zane. "I…" She trailed off under the influence of his cold stare.

Ian furrowed his brow. "Didn't your assistant say something about the US wanting your TV programme?"

"Yes, they do, but—"

"They'll love you. When does filming start?"

She shrugged. "I'm not sure."

A woman Zane had never seen before approached them,

with a camera in hand. "They want her as soon as they can get her, don't they, Rach?"

Before Rachel could answer, the woman had raised the camera and taken a snap of the three of them. Ian signaled over his own photographer and before Zane knew it he, Ian and Rachel had been photographed by someone who Rachel introduced as her agent. It became a melee as members of the public pushed forward, all wanting selfies with Rachel. Zane backed out as soon as he could and watched her. She gave that broad beautiful smile that lit up the whole room, but when she turned it to Zane he could see uncertainty in her eyes. But still the smile held. The disconnect between the two hit Zane. It was precisely what he hated. Feeling one thing on the inside and showing something else on the outside. *That* wasn't real. *That* wasn't what he wanted.

Without acknowledging Rachel, he thrust his hands in his trouser pockets and walked decisively away from the school, through the open gates and down the road toward the sea. He needed air. He needed to get away from things he'd thought he'd already left behind.

By the time Rachel had finished talking with Ian, and having her photo taken with scores of people from around the district, her heart and spirits had sunk to rock bottom.

Zane had disappeared. But more worrying than that was the way he'd looked at her from across that crowded hall—as if he were looking at a stranger. But not just a stranger, a stranger he didn't much like. She hadn't seen that expression on his face when she actually *had* been a stranger to him. *Then* he'd shown interest, humor and all the other lovely things she associated with him. But just now? Nothing.

As she helped clear up the hall, she was only vaguely aware

of the chatter of the other women. Why had Zane reacted as he did? She'd thought they were getting on so well. She'd imagined he'd be as impressed and happy to see her on stage as everyone else had been. Seemed he wasn't like everyone else. But hadn't she known that from the beginning? And hadn't that been the reason why she'd been so attracted to him?

As the last cooking implement was packaged up into a box, and loaded into the van to go back to Belendroit, she realized she'd stuffed up big time. Not only stuffed up, but created a disaster from which she wasn't sure her newly formed relationship with Zane would recover. He'd given her hints as to his feelings about fame and she'd totally underestimated their importance.

The rest of her team had returned to Christchurch and wouldn't be back until Monday when filming started, so she drove her father's van, loaded with her equipment, back to Belendroit early, pleading a headache. She covered the gamut of emotions on the short trip back to the homestead. From shock at Zane's reaction, through to anger at herself for being so upset and so vulnerable. She'd thought she'd moved on from the person she had been, but she'd thought wrong.

She pulled up in the drive of Belendroit and wearily got out. Her father wasn't there. At the school he'd been lapping up the compliments directed at her, and transforming them into compliments about himself. No doubt he was still there. He was in his element, surrounded by women and flirting outrageously with them all. Exactly as she'd done on stage, she thought grimly.

She was about to unload the contents of the van when she heard a noise. It was coming from the woods. She looked around but didn't see a car. She approached hesitantly, walking along a path which Zane had made sure was no longer overgrown, although the trailing creepers and vines still dangled from the towering trees overhead.

Then she saw him. Zane. He was finishing up some work he'd begun the previous weekend. His tools were piled neatly to one side whereas they'd been scattered last time she'd seen them. He hadn't heard her arrive. He continued digging up a tree which would complete the work in that area. She watched as he moved the dead wood back and forth until it came loose and he tossed it onto a pile. Passing his hand over his forehead, he went to pick up his things. He stopped in his tracks when he saw Rachel.

"Zane," she said, in as cool a tone as she could achieve. But even so it nowhere near matched Zane's earlier icy response.

"Rachel. I didn't think you'd be back here so quick. I thought you'd be out celebrating in Christchurch with the rest of your crew."

"No. I wasn't in the mood." She looked around, desperately trying to think of something neutral to say, something to engage him in conversation, something to prevent him from leaving. "You've been busy."

"I've come to finish up and collect my stuff. I didn't think you'd be here." His coolness brought about a familiar hurt, deep in the pit of her stomach. Another rejection. But this one hurt far more than any other. She balled her hands and swallowed it down. She refused to let this go the way of all her other relationships, without a fight.

"Or else you wouldn't have come," she said.

"That's not what I said."

"But it's what you meant, isn't it?"

He didn't answer. She walked toward him and stopped, folded her arms across her chest, and tilted her head to one side. "Tell me, what was it which pained you so?" She raised her hand to stop him from saying anything. "The sight of me in the public eye, putting on a performance, or was it that you hadn't known—that this was something which you hadn't organized, you hadn't controlled?" She was aware of the hint of anger in her voice but she didn't care anymore.

"What pained me was that I didn't recognize you."

She frowned. Out of all the answers he could have given, she hadn't anticipated this. "Didn't recognize me? Okay, I visited the hairdresser for the occasion and dressed smarter than usual, but... didn't recognize me? What do you mean?"

"Exactly that." She hadn't thought his voice could get any colder, but apparently it could. "On that stage you changed into a person I didn't know."

She shrugged. "I... I have different sides to my personality, I know I do. I've always enjoyed acting and that's all it is —an acting role. What's so sinister about that?"

"You seemed to be pretty much into it."

"I was. It's what I do. It's my job."

"I didn't know. I thought you were a chef."

"And *that*, you didn't mind. You could cope with the idea of me slaving in a kitchen, behind the scenes, but not me being out in front, where people liked to interact with me. That's it, isn't it? You were pissed that I was the center of attention."

"No, Rachel. What I was unimpressed with was how much you so obviously *enjoyed* being the center of attention."

"So? Is that a hanging offense?"

"It is in my book. It's the thin end of the wedge. Where does it end? What would you sacrifice to hang on to that feeling?"

"That's ridiculous."

"Maybe, but it's how I feel."

"So... you're not even grateful for the fact that you've raised all the money you needed to take your team away and then some?"

He closed his eyes briefly. "Of course I'm grateful. What you did today was"—he shrugged, as if he were having difficulty coming up with the right word—"was one of a kind. No one else could have managed it. I just didn't want that person to be you."

"Why? Tell me why?"

"I thought you'd join in with the mothers. I thought you'd have a cake stall or something. I had no idea you'd pull a stunt like this."

"This *stunt*, as you call it, has everyone else, but you, ecstatically happy."

"Then you should be pleased."

"No. I'm not."

"Why?"

"Because I did it for you. I wanted *you* to be happy. I wanted *you* to be pleased." She bit her lip to stop herself from saying the words that threatened to tumble out of her mouth, words that would give away precisely how much she'd come to feel for Zane in such a short space of time.

He reached out instinctively and took her hands in his. The cool was gone now, replaced by a wistful sadness. "You mistook me for someone else, Rachel. I was pleased to be with you before… more than pleased. I wanted nothing out of the ordinary. In fact it was only ordinary I wanted."

"And you thought you'd found it in me?" She shook her head in disbelief. "I'm not ordinary, Zane. I have no intention of *ever* being ordinary."

"I realize that now. I see that you won't fit into this life. You've another life waiting in the US for you which, for some reason, you haven't told me about. I thought you were here looking for a quiet life, a *real* life, but I was mistaken. Or maybe"—he dropped her hands—"that was simply another act, an act you thought would appeal to me."

She reeled back at the insinuation of his words. "Don't you dare talk to me like that."

He held up his hands in apology. "I'm sorry, I shouldn't

have said that. You have to understand, I *had* a life like that, played out in the public. I had a woman I thought loved me, and who I loved, and none of it was real. Take the fame away and everything else crumbled, fell away like a pack of cards. It was empty. Nothing there. I don't want that again. I want something real which I can build on."

"And so do I. But I can't stop being myself. What you saw back there is a real part of me. I can't suppress it. I enjoy it. But I want a change, too."

"But what about the States?"

"Before I think about that I'm contractually obliged to do half a dozen episodes under my current contract in New Zealand."

"So you *will* be leaving Akaroa, then, one way or another."

"No. Not yet. I've decided to film them here. At Belendroit. That's why I had all the equipment around which I used at the fundraiser. As to the US…" She shrugged defiantly. "I haven't decided yet."

He sighed. "Rachel, I'm sorry, I thought we had things in common, I thought we might…" He stopped himself short. "But there's no way I can have a replay of my old life. No way I can build a future on the values your world holds dear."

His words were harsh but his expression revealed a pain and confusion which touched Rachel, despite herself.

"You're still hurting, Zane Black! You need to get over it and understand that what you want—this *ideal* woman—isn't real. And that's exactly what I am—real—and I intend to stay that way. And if you don't like it then you know what you can do." She lifted her chin, her heart pounding with emotion. Part of her believed what she said, but a very tenacious small part also wanted to wrap her arms around him and show him exactly how real she was. For long seconds their gaze held—the only moving things were the foliage above them which shimmered in the breeze, and a couple of fantails who darted in and out of the sunlight catching flies. Then he shook his head and looked away.

She watched him collect his tools, waiting for him to say something more, racking her brains trying to think what she could say to stop this nightmare from continuing. But there was silence until he walked away without looking back.

"Zane!" He stopped walking but didn't turn around. She took a step forward. Her head was full of things she wanted to say, her body full of things she wanted to do, not least to fling her arms around that strong man and make him stay, make him see that he was wrong. She half-laughed at the notion of him walking away with her hanging on to his thighs, being dragged through the newly-cleared gardens. She forced down the hysteria born of frustration and anger.

He twisted his head toward her, but not so far that he could see her. It nearly broke her heart. And it made her sense of self plummet like never before. Maybe they'd all been right—all her exes—grinding her down. Maybe she wasn't worth much. Because of all the people whose opinions she respected, Zane had quickly become the most important.

"Yes?" he asked.

It was the last pin-prick to a bubble of hope she'd nurtured since she'd met him. "Nothing," she said softly, before turning and walking away from him.

EVEN WITHOUT LOOKING BACK at her after she'd called out, Rachel's expression was imprinted on Zane's mind. It haunted him with every step he took toward his car. He loaded up his garden tools and started the engine. He had to drive carefully as the two cocker spaniels came bounding down the drive ahead of Jim, barking madly. But he didn't stop, merely wound down the window and exchanged a few words. If he'd been asked afterwards what those words were, he wouldn't have been able to say.

He drove off over the winding road up the hill to the valley beyond, to the Maori land which had been in his tribe for centuries. As soon as he entered its boundary, he felt a sense of peace. He drove through the small community and out the other side to where his house stood slightly apart.

He walked out onto the veranda which overlooked the marae, and scanned the valley. The place was virtually empty. Of course everyone would be at the school, enjoying what was on offer. And so he should be too, as one of the teachers. He rarely shirked his duty but there was no way he could have stayed there listening and watching everyone idolize Rachel as if she were some kind of goddess. It was ridiculous, he thought as he placed his tools in his shed.

"Zane!" He looked up and saw his gran waving at him. Her arthritis must surely have been playing up if she didn't go to the school gala.

He waved and she beckoned. He looked around his place. He had things to do, and, besides, he wasn't in the mood for company. But who could deny his gran? Certainly not him.

He walked down the hill toward her cottage.

"Gran," he greeted, looking down at her—she seemed to get smaller with each passing month. But she was still sharp-eyed and held herself proudly, still wore the greenstone *taonga* around her neck. His gaze lingered on the pendant—a symbol of strength and beauty, so fitting for the women of his tribe. "Are you okay?"

She was shelling peas and had a pile of kumara beside her to peel. "Course I'm okay, boy. But someone's got to prepare tonight's *kai* while you lot are gallivanting about."

He looked at her knobbly hands and then at the peeler. "Let me do that."

"Sure, if you want to. But don't take pity on me. I'm not

alone, you know. The girls rigged up this TV screen for me. If I can't get to the school, then at least I can see her here."

It wasn't until he'd sat down that he realized who the 'her' was. A close up of Rachel filled the screen. He was transfixed by her beauty, her low melting voice, and her wicked wit which punctuated her monologue in exactly the right places. She was as sexy as hell.

He focused on peeling the kumara. The faster he finished the job, the sooner he was out of there.

"She's a beauty all right. A natural beauty," said his gran, consideringly.

He looked up at the TV. "What's natural about the way she flicks her hair back from her face?"

His gran chuckled. "Natural seduction, you could say, eh boy?"

He couldn't argue with that, not with the way his groin tightened and his eyes dropped to her full lips. He swallowed. "She's putting it on. She doesn't do that in real life."

Gran pointed to the TV. "*That's* not real life! You should know the difference by now. That's a performance, and a damn good one, too." She laughed again at Zane's expression.

"But it's so different to what she's like. Which one is her?"

Gran shrugged. "Probably both. Nothing wrong with a bit of complexity in a woman."

"Maybe. But it makes it hard to know which version to trust." He glanced once more at the screen.

"She hasn't changed much. Become more beautiful if anything."

That made him take his eyes off the screen. "You knew her?"

She glanced slyly at him. "Sure did. She was a cute kid."

He had nothing to say about that because he knew she probably had been.

"Some of the whanau used to hang around with her in town. Only saw her up here a few times, though."

"Who with?"

"Lisa and Tommy mainly."

"Oh." That would be right, Zane thought as he did the math. His step sister and step brother were around Rachel's age.

"Long time after you went to Auckland to be with your mother."

He winced and his gran reached out her hand and touched his arm. He looked up instantly. His gran wasn't a demonstrative woman; she was a tough one. "You did all right, lad. You did what you had to do and it made you the man you are today. A man I'm proud to call my *mokopuna*."

Zane couldn't remember his gran ever having said that she was proud he was her grandchild before. Her approval had always been implicit. He took another look at her. Maybe her age was making her sentimental.

"What's got into you, Gran? You raised us to be tough, remember? Not sentimental."

"I'm an old lady now, Zane, and I see things a little different. It's like I can see more, more about people, can see inside them, what's hurting them."

He grunted, uncomfortably. "So age has given you x-ray eyes. That's some super power."

"You can laugh if you like, and you can not believe me if you like." She shrugged. "Makes no difference to me. I'm simply saying I can see what your mother did to you. I can see its effect in the way you live your life, the hurt that's curled up inside you and that you protect, every minute of every day."

Zane froze, half way through peeling a kumara, the thick strip of peel caught mid curl. He stared at the orange vegetable, the sticky starch, white on his hands. He cleared his throat and finished peeling the kumara, then tossed it into the saucepan of water.

"What *you* have, Gran, is an imagination."

"Always had that, lad. Life's more fun with a bit of imagination. But I've always had my feet firmly on the ground, too, as you well know. And also, as you well know, I'm telling the truth. What I don't know is what you're going to do about it. I've been watching you since you returned, waiting for you to loosen up, but you haven't."

He plucked another kumara from the pile. "Loosening up isn't what I need, Gran. I've too many responsibilities."

"You can't look after everyone, boy. Not your kids in the school, not your whole family, nor your whole tribe. It's too much. Especially when you haven't looked after yourself first."

"I *do* look after myself."

"That's not what I mean. I mean when are you going to get yourself a girl?"

Involuntarily, his glance was drawn to the TV where Rachel was sipping the contents of a spoon. The peeler slipped and jabbed his finger. Damn.

"Yes, I heard you'd been seen with Rachel. She has her own issues of course, but she's a good girl. You could do worse."

"What issues? You mean the fact she's on TV for a living?"

Gran waved her hand dismissively. "Nah! If she hasn't told you then it's not up to me to tell you."

Zane's interest was piqued. He couldn't imagine what his gran was talking about but he knew better than to continue to quiz her.

"It doesn't matter anyway. Rachel's going to live and work in the US soon. And I'm staying here. I don't want anything to do with that kind of lifestyle."

"Not all girls are the same, my lad. I met your other lady,

the one you were engaged to, remember, and I knew she wasn't ever right for you."

"How? With those x-ray eyes of yours?" Zane rose. "It might have been nice if you'd told me."

"Sit down. You've more kumara to peel."

He sat. He might be in charge of students, might be on his board of trustees for his tribe, but if his gran told him to sit, he sat.

"Now, Rachel, she's different," continued his gran.

He bit his lip but didn't speak. It looked like he was going to have to sit through a Rachel-praising session whether he liked it or not.

"She's had her problems in the past."

Again he looked up at his gran, dying to know what these problems were, but, on seeing the look on her face, he knew he wouldn't get anywhere.

"But," she continued, "she's worked hard, made a success of herself. Now she's back, trying to sort herself out before moving forward once more."

"Gran, how do you know all this? Are you making it up?"

Gran simply tapped her forehead. "I have eyes, I can see."

"Not well, you can't," he couldn't help saying, after looking into Gran's rheumy eyes.

He received a sharp slap on his leg. "I may be old, but I'm not going to accept any of your cheek." She pointed a gnarled finger at him. "And you know exactly what I mean. She's here for a reason and it's not to try and tame that old man's garden."

"Jim's garden, you mean?"

"Yeah, that old man."

"He must be younger than you."

"Me and him clashed way back. We disagreed over something. No, Rachel's not here for him or his place."

"He's her dad, and it looks like she enjoys his company."

The old lady shrugged. "She's not here for him," she repeated firmly.

Despite himself, Zane's interest was caught. "So why do you think she's here?"

Gran's gaze held him levelly. For a moment Zane could almost believe she had x-ray vision. Then she picked up another kumara. "I reckon you'll find out soon enough."

"Doubt that. Rachel and I aren't seeing each other, no matter what the family says."

Gran smiled as if she knew different and rose to her feet with a stiffness which betrayed exactly how bad her arthritis was, and looked up into the sunshine. "It's been another glorious day on God's earth." She smiled.

What was it with old people? Zane mused as he carried the large pot of peeled kumara to a bench out of the sun. His grandmother had always been the pivot, the fulcrum of his world, the strong one, the wise one. Her feet had always been on the ground, and her reason had always been sound and based on logic. But over the last year or so, she'd been given to openly praising God and the world, as if what stood between her and the next world was so insubstantial that it was hardly there. She'd always gone to church, always abided by Christian teachings, but now? Her religion had become an everyday thing, a fundamental part of her.

He shrugged again and helped her up the path to the marae, to pass the afternoon away with the other elderly *kuia*, before going up the hill toward his own cottage.

He felt like he'd gotten to know a lot more about Rachel by watching her on the TV than he had by spending a week in her company. And, despite what his gran said, he wasn't sure he liked what he saw. He'd spent ten years living the life of a professional rugby player and all that that entailed—fast cars, beautiful women, media attention. And that was why he was where he was now: because he'd grown tired of the shallowness of that lifestyle. He'd wanted *real*. And the Rachel he was looking at on the TV was the opposite of that.

~

RACHEL GAVE a cursory knock on Gabe's front door before opening it. The narrow hallway was empty. She wandered through to the study where Gabe was practically knee-deep in paperwork.

"Thank God you're back," said Rachel, waving a bottle of wine at him.

He raised an eyebrow and dropped a pile of papers. "Good to see you, too."

Rachel walked into the kitchen and pulled open the cutlery draw, fishing around for a bottle opener. Gabe followed.

"So, why the drama, Rach?"

She cut off the top of the seal, and twisted the corkscrew into the cork, sending it in at an angle. "Why don't you have a modern corkscrew? They're so much easier," she grumbled.

Gabe reached out for it. "Give it here. If you've gone to the trouble of bringing such a good bottle of wine, the least I can do is make sure you don't get bits of cork in it."

Rachel opened the cupboards and withdrew two mismatched wine glasses. She held them up the light and screwed up her face. "Where on earth did you get these from?"

Gabe pushed aside his unruly hair and glanced at the glasses. "From the charity shop down the road."

Rachel tutted. "You're a doctor, for goodness sake. You earn enough to buy a decent wine glass or three."

He popped out the cork and poured the wine into the glasses, sending her a wry glance. "You're in a bad mood."

Rachel pushed her hand through her hair, accepting the

glass. "I'm in a *sad* mood, is what I'm in," she said quietly, taking a sip of wine.

"Hm," said Gabe, holding the wine up to the light as he swirled it around. "That doesn't sound so good."

"It's not. It's the opposite of good." She looked around. "I'm hungry. Have you any food?"

"No, I ate in Christchurch. If I'd known you were coming I'd have got something in. You should have told me yesterday when I rang home."

"I didn't know I was coming here yesterday."

"So what's happened today?" Gabe rummaged through the larder and found a family bag of chippies. He offered Rachel a bag and she tore it open and took a handful. She never ate chippies but today she didn't care.

"Everything," she muttered darkly through a mouthful. She grimaced at their tartness and checked the packet. "These could so be improved with less salt and toning down that... ugh, that unnatural flavor." She began reading through the list of ingredients in very small print on the back of the packet.

"I wouldn't do that, Rach."

She sighed. "You're probably right," she said, continuing to eat. She opened the french doors which led out into the small courtyard surrounded by the backyards of other houses and shops. Gabe threw out a couple of cushions and she sat down on the back door step.

He sat beside her, nudging her with his shoulder. "Good to see you, sis. Even if you are in a bad mood."

She smiled up at him. "I'm so glad you're back, Gabe. Everyone's been driving me crazy!"

"Amber?"

Rachel shook her head. "Amber's just Amber, living in Amber world, on Amber time."

"So nothing new there, then. And Dad?"

"Dad? We've been working in the garden, sorting out those dead trees but he doesn't seem very grateful."

Gabe paused. "We? As in Zane?"

She took another sip of wine and looked directly ahead, toward the back gate beyond which was a narrow alley and another backyard. "Zane and me."

"Zane and you, eh?"

She shot him a black look. "Yes."

"So why the bad mood?"

"We fell out. Seems he's not impressed about me being on the TV."

"Ohhh."

The way Gabe said "Oh" irritated Rachel. It was too long and all-knowing, as if what she'd said described something which Gabe understood perfectly. "It wasn't like that. It wasn't that kind of 'oh.'"

"What kind of 'oh' was it then?"

Rachel paused. "The 'oh' began as a surprised 'oh', quickly became kind of intrigued 'oh', and then…"

"Then?"

"Sort of changed into a happy sighing kind of 'oh' and then a sad 'oh'."

"That's a lot of different kinds of 'oh's in only a few short weeks," said Gabe.

"Yes. It's been that kind of month."

They sat in silence, sipping their wine. Rachel was waiting for Gabe to say something, to ask her more questions. And she'd be ready with a tirade. But Gabe said nothing. She let the silence lengthen and then shook her head.

"Gabe Connelly! You're my brother and I love you, but I'll never understand you. Why don't you say something? Any normal person would have asked me a dozen questions by now!"

"Would they?" Gabe asked mildly. "Then I guess I'm not normal."

"You're normal, all right. I just don't know whether it's lack of interest or some kind of professional thing which you employ with your patients, giving them time to tell you stuff."

He took another sip of the wine. "This is good wine."

"Gabe," she said in a warning tone.

He grinned. "And I *am* interested. Tell me, Rachel," he asked in a pseudo psychiatrist voice, "what appears to be the problem?"

"He's your mate, right? Zane, I mean."

"Sure is. I've known him for years. As a teenager he used to come back to the marae from time to time and I got to know him then. I lost touch with him when he was living the high life as an All Black, but I see a lot more of him now. He's a good guy."

"Then why doesn't he like me?" Rachel couldn't quite prevent her question sounding petulant. She pouted a little as she met Gabe's amused glance.

"I'm sure he likes you. Who wouldn't?"

"*Him* apparently."

"So… are you going to tell me exactly what happened?"

Rachel closed her eyes against the evening sunshine and leaned her head against the side of the doorpost. "We were getting on really well. We'd met quite a few times…and things were going great. He offered to help sort out the garden for Dad and in return I said I'd help out at the fundraiser at the school."

"So far so impersonal, but good."

"Oh…There was personal, too."

He raised his hand. "I don't want to hear about that. Tell me what happened next. Only the impersonal stuff."

"The fundraiser. Zane asked me to help out and I thought

I'd offer my services, you know, as me. I thought it would help everyone if I did what I usually do. You know…"

"Put on a performance."

"Exactly," said Rachel.

"But Zane doesn't like performances. It's not his style."

"Yeah, well, I didn't know that. Of course I do now. But I've no idea why. What's up? Why is he so weird about it?"

"You have to understand that Zane Black isn't like most other people. He sees life in two colors—black or white. He lived his version of the high life as an All Black which, believe me, was far tamer than any of his team mates. And he fell in love with a woman who wanted all that Zane's fame could bring her. Trouble was, he was in it for the game, and not for the glory. She left as soon as she realized that he had no interest in hanging around once he'd sustained his injury. He refused commentating jobs, TV work, the lot. That wasn't him. And unfortunately it *was* her. He was shattered when she broke off their engagement. And it's made him wary, I guess, of anything or anyone which smacks of pretense."

"And you think I smack of pretense?"

Gabe grinned. "Of course not. You're like Dad. You enjoy putting on a bit of a performance and there's nothing wrong with that. But you don't let it go to your head and you're as normal as me."

"I'm not *that* normal," said Rachel.

"Well, normal enough." Gabe took another sip of wine. "I can imagine how the rest played out. Zane discovered you mid-performance and decided the budding friendship was over."

"More or less. So what you're saying is that Zane now has me pigeonholed as a flake."

"Afraid so. But leave it with me, I'll talk to him."

"No!" Rachel said, alarmed. "I don't want you to say anything. Apart from the fact I'd feel like I was fourteen years old again, I reckon it was a narrow escape. If he's going to take on like this whenever he discovers a side of me which surprises him, then I'm best off without him."

Gabe put his arm around his sister. "Rach, you're a wonderful woman and I'm sure Zane recognized that from the moment he first saw you. But you got him in a place that's still hurting and vulnerable and you scared the devil out of him. That's all. He'll come round."

"I'm not sure I want him to," she said, pouting once more, ever such a little.

"I reckon you do, otherwise you wouldn't be here plying me with wine and getting me to talk about him."

"True." She grinned. "So tell me about him."

Gabe winced. "Are you sure you want me to?"

"Yes. Of course. Why wouldn't I?"

"There's something else, Rach, that I didn't mention. I was going to but then I heard how good you two were getting on, and I changed my mind."

"About what?"

"About telling you."

"Gabe! What were you worried about telling me?"

He placed his glass of wine deliberately on the table and looked at her with a seriousness he usually reserved for his patients. Rachel's heart plummeted.

"Tell me, Gabe."

"I know you hate talking about what happened to you when you were sixteen. I realize I'm probably the only one of us who knew. We were too close for me not to know, even though you were swept off to Wellington for a 'holiday'. A six-month holiday. A holiday from which you returned, a changed girl." He paused. "The father of your child... Tommy Tau?"

Rachel licked her lips and nodded.

"He's Zane's half-brother."

5

---

*R*achel twisted the old-fashioned cord around her finger as she leaned back against the kitchen wall. "Surely it's not too late to re-arrange things?" She glanced at the boxes of equipment which stood ready to be unpacked. "There's only two…" She peered at the pile of boxes stacked on the veranda. "Or three boxes…or more," she murmured as an afterthought.

She pulled the phone away from her ear. Her assistant wasn't impressed with her last-minute attempt to change locations for her final shoots back to Wellington. Suddenly, filming at Belendroit had lost its appeal. She wanted nothing more than to get away. At least in Wellington, people didn't have a go at her for being good at her job. But it seems it was too late.

"Okay, okay. We'll carry on as arranged."

She winced as she was forced to listen to another tirade from her harassed assistant before replacing the old bakelite phone on the hook with a light ding.

She could do it, she said sternly to herself as she opened the box and pulled out some pans. It wasn't as if Zane was going to willingly cross her path after the fundraiser debacle. She simply had to stay out of his way. Because there was no way she wanted to get together with a man who not only thought she was some kind of superficial showgirl but would despise her for giving up her child, and not just any child, but his own brother's. Something, she knew, which the family-oriented Zane would most definitely not approve of.

No wonder she'd thought she recognized Zane when she'd first seen him. He and her first boyfriend might have different mothers, different surnames, courtesy of Zane's beloved step-father, but they had the same birth father. Like it or not, Zane was her daughter's uncle.

Her daughter... a girl, she had to admit, who he must know, even if he didn't know Rachel was her mother. She leaned against the kitchen bench, gripping the cool surface for strength.

But maybe he'd understand. After all she'd been so young and had only done what she'd thought right, what would be best for her daughter. But even as she thought these things, she had an image of Zane at the marae, caring for all the youngsters and old alike. And she realized that the decision she'd made would be totally alien to him. He'd understand why she'd done it, but he wouldn't approve, and she doubted he'd forgive.

"What a mess," she muttered.

"What's a mess?" asked Gabe, as he entered the kitchen. "Not your food, I assume." He opened the fridge, took out a chicken leg and began eating. "No," he said with his mouth full. "Definitely not your cooking."

"What are you doing here at this hour anyway? Shouldn't you be working?"

"I've been on a home visit and was passing so I thought I'd drop in."

"To eat the contents of our fridge?"

"No. To invite you to dinner." He walked over to the door. "Tonight. Five-thirty my place."

"Five-thirty? That's not dinner, that's…"

But there was no point finishing her sentence because Gabe hadn't waited for an answer and was already walking across the grass to his car. "See you later then," he called before getting into the car.

Rachel drummed her fingers on a copper bottomed pan as she watched her kind, but interfering, brother roar off down the road in his old bomb of a car.

Gabe never invited her to dinner in such a formal way. His was an open house for her and their family, always had been and, she hoped, always would be. Gabe's lack of private life was public knowledge, not that he seemed to mind. Rachel sometimes wondered if he minded anything. If he did, he hid it well. Whatever Gabe's reason for inviting her, she was glad. She was tired of being alone with her own thoughts which refused to stop tormenting her.

WITH DINNER PREPARED for her father who declined to join her and Gabe, she left her father happily sorting out his drinks cabinet which he seemed to think would be required when the place was descended on by the film crew the following week. She walked the twenty minutes to Akaroa, along the water front. She made a detour down Rue Jolie past the school and the adjoining field where some boys were kicking a ball around. She looked away again, annoyed with herself for her obsession, and turned down Church Street toward the old Telegraph Office which was now Gabe's home and practice.

The stone building with its ornate arch and pediment over the front door was an incongruous choice for Gabe, who was modest to a fault. But the door and the two large sash windows, which sat either side, opened up directly onto the pavement and had an amazing sea view. A window was invariably wide open from which, out of practice hours, music generally flowed, as it did now. It suited Gabe because he liked people, and he liked to live amongst them, even if he did live on his own.

Rachel raised her hand to give a cursory knock on the door but the door opened before her hand hit the varnished wood.

"Beat you to it." Gabe grinned. He stood two one side, one hand clutching a file which barely contained a bundle of obviously unsorted papers.

Rachel gave Gabe a kiss on the cheek and lifted his hand with the overflowing file. "When are you going to get yourself an assistant?"

"When I find someone who can do the job without trying to organize me, too."

Rachel proceeded through to the comfortable lounge which also served as a study and opened out onto the small courtyard. "By organize, I'm guessing you mean want to marry you."

"Twice it's happened in the last six months, would you believe?" He dumped the pile of papers onto another pile on top of his desk.

"I would. You're a nice guy."

He mumbled something and poured her a glass of wine.

"Isn't it a bit early for wine?"

He passed her hers and poured himself one and took a sip. "No."

"Care to elaborate?"

"You'll see."

Butterflies danced in her stomach. "So, you *are* up to something."

"Mrs. Jones put a crockpot on and prepared some veggies." He took another swig, glanced at the clock and reached for his jacket.

Rachel jumped up. "Where are you going?"

He shrugged. "House call or something."

"Gabe!" But before he'd a chance to escape, there was a brief knock at the door, followed by the sound of the door opening, and footsteps coming towards them. Zane stepped into the room, looking as shocked as she felt.

"Zane, good to see you, mate," said Gabe. "I have to leave now. But I'm sure my sister will entertain you until I get back."

Rachel glared at Gabe who didn't even have the decency to look embarrassed.

Zane took one look at Rachel and placed a six-pack of beer on the table and stepped away again. "Look, Gabe, I'll come back another time."

"Not at all. Dinner's ready and Mrs. Jones would be deeply hurt if you didn't try her beef casserole. She made it especially for you." He hesitated, before deciding more persuasion was needed. "She's very fond of you, you know. She asked that you tell her whether you liked it with the tomatoes." Gabe cleared his throat, obviously making it up as he went along. "Or not."

Rachel shook her head in disbelief. Gabe knew Zane would have done a 360 and walked straight out if it was left up to him. And he also knew that Zane's reluctance to hurt anyone—especially Mrs. Jones—would make him stop in his tracks, at least long enough to let Gabe get away.

Gabe shot Rachel a half-apologetic, half-hopeful look. Maybe it was for the best, thought Rachel. It would give Zane a chance to apologize.

"And you wouldn't want to lie to Mrs. Jones when you see her at school tomorrow, would you, Zane?" asked Rachel with a smile. As well as being devoted to Gabe, Mrs. Jones was a dinner lady at the school and notoriously fierce.

"Anyway, I'll see you guys later. I... have to go." Gabe left the house, banging the door shut, and walked up the street.

"Doesn't sound as if your brother needs a car to go to his next appointment."

"No. I'm guessing his appointment is taking him to the pub up the road for his dinner."

Zane stuck his hands in his pockets and looked around uncomfortably. "He's never pulled anything like this on me before."

"Me neither. I guess there's a first time for everything." She chewed her lip indecisively. "Can I get you a glass of wine?"

"Bit early isn't it?"

She laughed. "That's what I said. But, to be honest, I think Gabe has something there. I think I need one."

"Me, too. Except make mine a beer."

Her hand shook slightly as she poured a glass of beer for Zane. She was conscious of the space he occupied in the room. He was like one giant mass of energy, sexual energy at that. She had the strange feeling she was being drawn to him. That if she let down her guard, she'd physically sway toward him. Ridiculous! As she handed him his drink, their fingers brushed and she jumped back as if burned.

"Is everything all right?" Zane asked.

She shrugged and walked determinedly back to the kitchen bench and took hold of her wine, her other arm wrapping defensively across her waist. "As all right as anything is when you feel you've been tricked by your brother."

"We don't have to do this, you know, not if you don't want to."

"No, it's fine. I'd quite like to hear you apologize."

"Me, apologize? I thought you were."

Rachel rolled her eyes, placed her drink back on the kitchen bench and walked toward the door. "Then maybe we should quit right now."

Rachel got as far as Zane before he reached out and touched her arm. It was a gentle touch, but it might as well have been a metal trap, because there was no way she could move. She was aware only of the heat of his touch against her naked arm.

"Look, Rachel, this is crazy stuff. Gabe's right. We need to clear the air."

She looked up from under her long lashes, her default expression when trying to hide her thoughts. Perhaps Zane really did feel something for her. "Maybe."

"I mean," Zane continued. "We'll be seeing each other around Akaroa until you leave, so we may as well make it as easy for ourselves as possible."

"Oh," she said, unable to conceal the disappointment. "Of course." She was getting hotter and more flustered by the minute. Rachel Connelly, professional chef and show business personality, *never* got flustered. "Let's go outside, shall we?"

Without waiting for an answer she pushed open the doors and sat on one of the wrought iron chairs grouped around a table under a sheltering arbor of pink and white jasmine. In an effort to improve their appearance, Amber had painted the rusting chairs pink, despite Gabe's protests. But he had a hopelessly soft spot for his little sister and pink they remained. Pink, but still uncomfortable and rickety. Gabe probably hadn't noticed as he preferred to sit on the doorstep. Zane sat, looking too large for the delicate chair, and spectacularly ill at ease.

Rachel was determined not to be the first one to speak. If he was still expecting an apology from her then he had a long wait ahead of him. She looked steadily across the small brick courtyard, through which tufts of alyssum and straggling weeds emerged, toward the hills, just visible above the fence. The silence lengthened and she took another sip of wine and crossed her legs, jiggling them in irritation.

Then Zane placed his hand on her knee and she jumped, lifting her startled gaze to his calm, resigned one.

"Rachel, stop jiggling. You're driving me nuts."

"I'll jiggle if I want to," she said, trying to force her leg to move, which it now proved quite unwilling to do.

He took his hand from her leg and she wondered if it would be inappropriate of her to take it and place it back where it belonged again. She decide that, on balance, it would.

"It's just that I want to apologize and the sight of your skirt shifting up your leg is proving distracting."

"Oh." She pulled her dress down a little. Her leg was no longer jiggling.

He brought his chair around to face her. "I'm sorry, Rachel. I've been an idiot. All you've been guilty of is doing what you agreed to do, and more."

"That's what I thought you asked me to do."

"Yes, I realize that now. But I had no idea about what you really did for a living."

"That makes it sound shady. Like I have some illegal business on the side."

"I guess I made it sound shady, because that's how I feel about the world of celebrity. I hate it. I hated living it as an All Black, I hated seeing what it did to the celebrities themselves, and I hated seeing what it did to people who hung on their every word and action, and thought and deed. It's a shallow life which brings out the worst in people. People pretend things they don't feel so they can be a part of that world."

"I know it *can* be like that, Zane, and I've been used like that, like you have, by the sounds of things. But you live and learn a little, and there are parts of my job I absolutely love. It's fun for one thing, it's educative for another, and, yes, I guess I enjoy being a bit of a showgirl, putting on an act." She shrugged. "It doesn't make me shallow. Think of it as a kind of amateur dramatics, like Dad enjoys—the kind of comedy farce which The Little Theatre puts on during the summer."

"I over-reacted." He shot her a rueful smile.

"Yes. *And* some. I mean, you did tell me about your ex and how she liked the limelight and how *you* didn't. But I hadn't imagined it would have such a drastic effect on you."

He grunted. "It's all or nothing with me."

"But"—she grimaced and looked up at him—"life's not really like that though, is it? People aren't black and white, and nor are situations." He didn't answer and she thought he had simply dismissed her remark. "I mean…I *do* understand. I've been in the same situation and it turns your world upside down, doesn't it?" Still no response. "Makes you doubt everything, including yourself. *Especially* yourself."

He settled a narrowed, assessing gaze on her. "I've never doubted myself."

"Well, lucky you."

"And I don't know why you doubt *your*self. You're an intelligent, charming, beautiful woman. Why would you?"

She grinned. "Tell me that again and I might answer you."

He tipped his head to one side and shook it. "I'd like to know the answer to my question."

She sucked in a steadying breath. "Okay. There's other stuff that's gone on in my life, other things which I now realize have caused a certain amount of self-destructive behavior."

Zane's frown deepened. "What do you mean, self-destructive?"

"Nothing like drugs. I'm way too frightened of that stuff to do anything like that. No, I mean in terms of the choices I've made with men. It's like, I knew they were doomed from the beginning. I knew they didn't want me for who I was, because I didn't like me, particularly."

"That's ridiculous! You're one of the loveliest people I've ever met. I mean I know we haven't known each other long, but I can tell. I've experienced enough in my life to know bullshit when I hear it, and to recognize quality when I see it." He squeezed her hand. "And you're definitely quality."

She tore her gaze from his and rose from the chair. But before she could move away, she realized he was still holding her hand and he didn't seem to be in a hurry to let it go.

"Rachel, don't turn away from acknowledging how good you are. You should accept the compliment for the truth it is. You should accept it, and know it, and believe it. Only then can you move forward."

She pressed her lips together to stop them from quivering. No one had said such things to her before. Her brothers had tried, but it had never come out right. Her sisters also had, but they were her sisters, weren't they?

"Okay. Cool. I can do this. I'm… *quality*." She grinned. "I like that. It sounds like I should have a red sash with a seal of approval on it."

He laughed. "You should." Then his smile fell. "You should treat yourself like a most treasured object. Hold yourself gently, ensure you're always safe and regarded tenderly."

She exhaled. "You don't talk like a sports coach."

He grinned. "I do when I'm on the field. But now isn't the time for yelling at you to get out of the mud and carry on." He brushed his thumb over the back of her hand he still held. "Although, on second thoughts, it might be worth a try."

Rachel laughed. "I think I prefer the 'tender regard' speech better."

He stood up and brushed his hands lightly up her arms before resting them on her shoulders. "Have we sorted it, Rachel? Have you forgiven me for being such a complete and utter fool as to be angry with you when all you'd done was your very best to please me and the school?"

She cocked her head to one side. "I reckon. But maybe all that you said to me, you should say back to yourself. Maybe you haven't recovered from your breakup with your ex as well as you think you have."

"Oh, I have. She's past, long gone."

"But you run from anyone who reminds you of her."

"Okay, you probably have a point. It was an instinctive reaction. But I know better than to do that again."

"Do you? Why's that?"

"Because," he said, lifting her chin upwards. "I won't be able to do this." His kiss was as gentle and as tender as if he were treating her like the treasure he called her. It melted her from the lips down, until she thought her legs would give way. A problem which was sorted by Zane placing his hands firmly around her until he was supporting her with his arms and his body. No one had a right to taste so good, or kiss so good, Rachel thought lazily as she met his tongue along her lips with her own. Any thought of a brief kiss disappeared as her mouth opened under his like a flower at its first glimpse of sunlight. She wanted all he had to offer, as if she'd suffered too long under a long dark winter and was cold and needy for warmth and love.

Any last remaining traces of anger, resentment or confusion evaporated under the heat of his kiss. She wanted to dissolve under its intensity, wanted to become one with him desperately. It wasn't until he pulled away that she realized how much she wanted this, and how close she'd moved to him. Her hips were pressed against his. She didn't even remember leaning into him. Her body had responded of its own accord. She tried to pull away but his hands moved over her butt, keeping her firmly in place as he kissed her once more, and any thought of moving away vanished.

With the firm, commanding feel of his hands against her body, his mouth taking control of hers and his unmistakable arousal pressed against her belly, it was all she could do to stay standing. She felt he could have done anything to her then and she'd have been a willing party to it. As he pulled away once more, his eyes roving her face, his lips kissing her ear and her neck, she whimpered with desire.

"Christ..." he murmured against her neck.

"Kiss me again," she said.

There was a clatter of garden furniture way too close. Both of them pulled apart and looked over the brick wall.

"Hey, you two, there's a time and a place for that and it's not in the backyard while I'm trying to eat fish and chips!" The disgruntled neighbor glared at them, wrapped up his dinner and took it inside his house, slamming the door as he went.

They fell, laughing, against each other. He lifted her chin.

"I don't know how Gabe stands it," she whispered. "He doesn't seem to care about privacy."

"Well, I do. Maybe we should continue inside?"

She nodded and he grabbed her hand and they went inside and closed the door. They got no further than the door, against which Rachel was pinned by Zane's arms, as his mouth found hers in yet more passionate kisses. When they finally came up for air, they fell onto the couch, their mouths finding each other's once more, their arms holding each other tight as if each feared the other would escape.

Eventually, Zane pushed Rachel's hair back from her face, his gaze sweeping her eyes, her nose, and her lips, his thumb pressing over her lower full lip, exactly where his own lips had so recently been. He rose and pulled her to her feet. "Now, where's this food Gabe promised?"

"Food? You want food?"

He grinned and put his arm around her waist and brought her hard against him. "You know what I want." He glanced down at the couch. "But I'm not going to make love to you on a friend's settee, immediately after a misunderstanding. I *will* make love to you, and when I do, it'll be more than a tumble on someone else's couch. Remember... a treasure, to be respected and treated tenderly."

"Tenderly?" She drew her finger down the outline of his face, so strong and so restrained. "You know, I liked it when you first said that word. But now I'm thinking, 'masterfully' would be closer to what I want."

He raised an eyebrow. "You'll find I'm capable of both."

He kissed her lightly on the lips, his nose nuzzling hers before pulling away. "Now, woman," he muttered. "Fetch me my dinner."

She shook her head with a smile. "If that's your idea of masterful, I'll stick with tender."

He cupped her face in his hands. "Rachel, I don't want it to be a passing thing, I want it to be special. And in my experience, the best way for that to happen is to take is slowly." He glanced at the crockpot. "Slow cooking is the best and so is slow romance."

She put her head back and laughed. "I've never heard anyone compare slow cooking cheap meat until it's tender, to a romance."

"If slow can transform stringy meat into tender, imagine what it can do to already tender feelings."

She stopped laughing. "You have tender feelings toward me?"

"Uh-huh." He toyed with her hair. "Is that so hard for you to understand?"

"Yes, it is actually."

And for all her complaint about going slowly, she was pleased. Zane was different to anyone else she'd known and that could only be a good thing.

"Then you'd better get used to it."

"Okay, I can do that. Providing"—she brought his head around to face hers—"you don't compare me to a piece of stringy meat again."

He shook his head. "You are deliberately misunderstanding me." His hands slid down her curves. "And besides, that description would be entirely inaccurate."

She took a deep breath and pulled away, automatically taking her place behind the kitchen bench, while Zane slipped onto a stool. She took the lid off the crockpot and inhaled the smell. "Mrs. Jones has outdone herself this time."

Zane leaned on the bench toward Rachel and threaded his fingers through hers, drawing her to him and kissing them. "And so has Gabe."

"Brothers!" said Rachel. "They are pains in the butt but I wouldn't be without them."

"Me neither," said Zane. "Family always comes first."

Rachel's smile dropped as she watched Zane rummage through the drawers until he found the cutlery and took out a couple of knives and forks. They may have reconciled their differences this time. Zane may have wrenched himself away from his firmly-held black and white beliefs, this time. But the mention of his brother reminded her why Zane might change his mind about her being such a treasure. Family first...

Should she tell him and finish it before it began? But maybe he'd understand. Maybe, before he found out, their relationship would deepen, and be strong enough to withstand the truth. And... maybe, just maybe, Zane might lead her to her daughter.

~

GABE CLOSED the door and walked down the hallway. After the pub he'd gone to Belendroit to see his father and ended up staying much later than he'd imagined. He'd walked home, thinking about Zane and Rachel. They'd be good for each other. He hoped they'd managed to work things out before the evening was over. He'd been surprised that he hadn't seen Rachel but maybe she'd returned to Zane's house.

So when he stopped at the end of the hallway and looked into his kitchen-diner, he let out a laugh of surprise to see Zane and Rachel, fast asleep, fully clothed, in each other's arms, in front of the open window through which stars could be seen. Rachel's head rested on Zane's chest, and Zane's arms held her close. For some reason it moved Gabe and he took a step back. To see his old mate Zane, usually so dignified and private, like this—so unguarded—didn't seem right. But he couldn't take his eyes off them. Gabe's instinct had been right. These two *were* meant for each other. But, knowing a little of each other's past and personalities, he wasn't so sure it would be an easy road. He retraced his steps down the hall and opened the door and closed it loudly, rattling the colored panes of glass around the door. Then he clattered around in the hall and went into the bedroom and switched on the radio to give them a few minutes before he emerged into the kitchen.

"You two! I didn't think you'd still be here." Zane and Rachel stood apart in the kitchen like two guilty, but sleepy, teenagers, caught in the act. "I guess it was my wonderful dinner that put you to sleep," said Gabe, too heartily, wishing they'd return to normal. He didn't know how to act in these circumstances. Give him a complaint of the body and he could fix it, but this love stuff... Aside from bringing people together and feeding them, something his mother had taught him, he had no idea what to do.

"It was great," said Zane and Rachel simultaneously. They looked at each other and smiled.

"Good, good. Then maybe you'd let me get to bed. I've an early surgery in the morning."

"Sure." Zane stepped forward. "Thanks, mate."

Rachel followed Zane down the hall and stopped at Gabe, put her arms on his shoulders and went on tiptoe and kissed his cheek. "Thanks, Gabe." She smiled and walked away.

He watched them both leave and close the door behind them. He shut his eyes briefly, as a strange emptiness filled him at the sight of two people who were obviously hot for each other. He had plenty of offers from local girls to keep him company at night but he never took them up on it. Not that he wasn't tempted, but Akaroa was a small place and he held a very public position in it. Plus... he'd never been *really* tempted. The women had been similar to *him*—obvious and to the point. What you saw was what you got. It was mystery which always hooked him. And you didn't see many beautiful, mysterious women coming to his surgery, or the pub, for that matter.

He sighed and switched out the lights. No point hankering after what you couldn't have.

6

*R*achel had received no objections from her father about filming at Belendroit. He loved the idea of the house filled with people. As far as he was concerned he'd be hosting a big party, the more people, the better.

And there had certainly been a lot of people at Belendroit that morning. It had been over-run with people—cars and vans were parked in front of the house and down the side of the drive, backing up to the road. A tent had been erected to house surplus furniture from the house which had been replaced with pieces brought from Wellington. "Only to freshen and enhance the ambience," said the producer. And while Jim grumbled, Rachel had to admit that the additions, once they'd got them all moved into place, would make the kitchen look stunning.

However, without her usual team to handle the details, the hired hands from Christchurch had piled back into the van and driven off before the work was done and before Amanda, the show's producer, noticed.

"Where have they gone?" shrieked Amanda.

Jim sipped his coffee and looked at her over his half-spectacles. "Back to Christchurch, I should imagine."

"But they haven't finished. We need them to set things up! What are we going to do with all of this?"

"Don't look at us," the cameraman and lighting director said together. "We're too busy."

"Rachel!" said Amanda accusingly. "Any ideas? You bought us to this God-forsaken place."

Rachel rolled her eyes and shrugged an apology at Jim who didn't seem to be at all bothered as he offered unwanted advice to the lighting director. Amanda was brilliant at her job but less brilliant when things didn't go so well.

"We don't need all this stuff, Amanda. Let's make do with what we have."

One quick look around and Amanda was adamant. "No way."

Rachel thought of Gabe, but he was busy. In fact none of her brothers were around. And she refused to let her father help out as he wasn't as strong as he used to be. She shook her head. "We'll live with it until the guys come back tomorrow."

Amanda stalked outside on the veranda and looked around, hands on hips, as if hoping someone would appear as if by magic. And he did. She pointed into the bushes.

"What about your gardener? He looks like he could shift a thing or two single-handedly."

Rachel frowned. "Gardener? We don't have a..." She followed Amanda out onto the veranda and saw Zane between the trees, hacking away at a tree root.

"What about *him*?" Amanda repeated. "He'd be able to lug the big stuff around, wouldn't he?" Sean, the cameraman, glanced over, pushed himself off the wall with a lazy movement and placed the mug on the table. "I'll go and call him in."

"No!" said Rachel.

Sean held up his hand. "It's okay. I'll make it worth his while. People like him don't earn much doing stuff like that."

Before Rachel could remonstrate, someone else claimed her attention and she was up to her ears in sound tests and discussions with the set designer about the best placement of her kitchen range. There was something about the familiarity which was comforting. After years of doing this kind of work, Rachel sank back into it like she was pulling on worn comfy shoes. It was the best bit about the job, the cooking, the set up, the camaraderie with the people. Except... She glanced out the window at where Sean had to raise his hand against the sun to meet Zane's gaze. Zane stood with his arms relaxed at his side, his stance strong, his dislike obvious. Rachel half-laughed, changing it into a cough as she spoke to her assistant. Time to go rescue a situation.

Rachel walked up to the two men. She ignored Sean. "Hi, Zane. How's it going?"

He smiled. "Good thanks, Rachel. You?"

She grimaced. "Yeah, I got caught up in work over the past few days. Belendroit looks a bit different now, doesn't it?" She followed his glance at the newly painted deck and new tubs from which fresh flowers tumbled.

"Looks as if it's come direct from the interior of a lifestyle magazine."

"You see," said Amanda triumphantly, joining them. "It worked."

Zane raised an eyebrow as Amanda and Sean walked back to the house.

"So... are you enjoying it?" Zane asked.

"Yes, I am. I hadn't thought I'd enjoy it quite so much. There's something about being in the place I belong and doing the work I love."

"The place you belong? I haven't heard you say that before."

Rachel felt equally surprised she'd uttered the words. "I'm not sure I've *said* that before. But that's how I feel."

Zane was about to step closer to her. She knew he was going to kiss her, she could see it in his eyes and for a moment she forgot where she was, what she was doing and knew that *this* was exactly where she should be.

Then Sean re-appeared on the veranda. "Hey, Rach," he called across the garden. "So will your... *friend*...come and help move some stuff around? We'll make it worth his while."

Zane didn't even look at Sean or acknowledge that he'd spoken. He focused instead on Rachel. "Is this the guy you were telling me about?" Zane asked.

Zane didn't even care if Sean heard what he was saying.

Rachel shook her head. "No. That's Sean." She smiled uncomfortably at Sean who shook his head and looked away. "The guy I told you about is nothing to do with my work anymore."

"This one doesn't look so flash either."

Rachel grinned and looked at Sean, who was wiping imaginary dirt off his immaculate white shirt. "He's okay. He knows his job."

"Pity he doesn't know how to lift anything heavier than a clipboard. Are you sure you're okay with all of this?"

Rachel shrugged. "There were some contractual obligations I couldn't get out of. So I thought I'd bring the cameras to me, here. I thought it would be better."

"Better for whom?"

She swallowed. Somehow, from Zane's unsmiling expression, she got the impression he wasn't overly pleased with her decision.

"Better for Rachel, of course!" interrupted Sean. "And better for *you*, too, if you're willing to help out." Sean pulled out a wallet and started peeling hundred dollar bills out. He waggled a bundle at Zane. "Will this do?"

Zane glanced at Sean and then looked at Rachel. "Looks like your friend wants me to work for him. Do you want me to?"

"Not if you don't want to."

"I didn't say that. I asked what *you* wanted."

"Rachel, darling," interrupted Sean, "for God's sake tell him you need him to move some of your junk around. Otherwise we'll never get started."

"Zane, if you can help that would be great. But only if you've time. I don't want to impose on you."

Zane looked across at Sean. "Sure," he called out. "Make it worth my while and I'm your man."

The way Sean grinned and eyed Zane up and down made Zane shake his head. As he turned away he said to Rachel. "You owe me, Ms. Connelly."

"Happy to, Mr. Black."

Sean rolled his eyes, as Zane and Rachel walked up the steps onto the veranda. He thrust the money into Zane's hands and walked off. "I'll leave him to you."

She looked at the money and he followed her gaze. "My nieces will appreciate the extra money to waste on clothes the next time they're in Christchurch. So, what is it I'm meant to do?"

"Sean and the set designer think some of the furniture isn't right for the brand so want it moved out the way."

"And your Dad's okay with all of this?"

"Are you kidding? Dad's in his element, chatting up the women, charming the men. But are you sure you don't mind? I feel terrible, Zane. Really, I hope Sean wasn't rude to you?"

"Oh, he was. But I'm not so insecure as to let it worry me." He propped the spade up against the wall, and brushed his hands together. "Okay, lead on. Show me what the hired hand needs to do."

The next hour sped by as the team raced to finish off the

kitchen and adjoining sitting room to Amanda's precise specifications while Rachel focused on the food. Five minutes before filming began, Amanda walked around, running her fingers over the old-fashioned counter, lifting up things and putting them back in the wrong place. "You know, we could work with this. Change things up a bit. Rachel's Country Kitchen, or something like that. What do you think, Sean?"

Sean finished scanning a clipboard, signed it and looked up. "Rachel's *Grungy* Kitchen, if you ask me."

"Hey!" said Rachel sharply. "This is my family home, *my* show and I'd appreciate you keeping your comments to yourself."

Sean rolled his eyes. "For Christ's sake, what's got into you? We're filming in a few minutes. Got that?" Before Rachel could answer he'd moved off.

Amanda folded her arms and looked around the kitchen, tapping her beautifully manicured nails on her tanned arm. She walked up to Rachel who looked at her sideways as she tried to focus on arranging the ingredients as she wanted them. "You know, I think it would go well. We could use other parts of the house, too. It has great charm."

"I thought you didn't like it."

"What I like isn't relevant. The audience will like it. I feel it. We could do this as a regular gig."

"I don't want to."

"You should think about it." She glanced at Sean who'd moved outside. "Sean's replaceable. *You're* not."

Rachel shook her head in disbelief as Amanda went outside and began chatting to Sean as friendly as anything, as if she hadn't suggested that Rachel should sack him.

"Where do you want this?" Zane lifted a wooden free-standing chopping block with ridiculous ease.

"Sorry! Here, please."

Zane placed it where she wanted it and smoothed his hand over its surface. "Looks brand new."

"That's because it is. We don't have anything like this here."

"That's probably because you don't need it." Zane glanced at the others busy outside, going through the schedule. "I only want to know one thing, Rachel. How come you let them treat you like that? You're intelligent, talented, not to mention beautiful, and yet you let them boss you around like that? As if you're nothing?"

"I…" Rachel shrugged. "I don't know. It's their job to control various aspects of the programme."

"Maybe. But it's not their job to control *you*. You're worth more than that and I don't know why you can't see it."

Zane didn't wait for an answer and Rachel wasn't capable of giving one anyway. She watched him walk over to the veranda where Sean, busy on the phone, indicated with a wave of his hand which piece of furniture should go where. She knew it didn't bother Zane because Zane had no interest or respect for people like Sean. Zane was quite clear about why *he* was doing this—it was for her. But why was *she* doing this? Only a few more programmes and then the contract would be over. And then? Did she really want to leave all of this and go to the States?

Once filming was underway they only had a few short breaks to warn Jim to stop talking to someone. In the end, after a third interruption, the attractive second assistant was given the task of occupying Jim away from the set.

As the last bit of filming was complete, and the director called "it's a wrap", Rachel wiped her hands on a towel, leaned back against the kitchen bench and beamed.

"You enjoyed that, didn't you? I mean *really* enjoyed it," said Amanda, passing Rachel a glass of Champagne.

"Yeah," said Rachel warily. "I did."

"It came across in the way your hands held the bench, like they'd done it many times before, in the easy way you unhooked the implements from the pot holder, knowing the order amidst the chaos there. It was obvious it was your home and it worked. It was very relatable. I reckon that was your best performance yet."

Rachel looked at Amanda nervously. Amanda never looked thoughtful but she sure did now. "Amanda... what's on your mind?"

"You know what's on my mind, Rach. And as the day went on, my initial thoughts were only confirmed. You work well here. The footage shows it and the viewing audience will confirm it. I've been around this industry long enough to know a star performance when I've seen it."

"But there's the States."

Amanda shrugged. "Sure, you can go there if you want to. I know you needed to get away and that's why you agreed initially. But, in truth? The Americans would go for this like a shot. We could film the series here and have it syndicated to the US and around the world."

"But I don't know how long I'm going to stay here."

"I could give you another good reason to stay." Rachel followed Amanda's gaze to Zane who walked past, carrying something which looked far too heavy for a man to carry single-handedly. Amanda winked at Rachel. "See what I mean?"

She walked off, leaving Rachel watching Zane drop the piece of furniture where he thought it should go, rather than where Sean had told him to put it. Zane then ignored Sean and brushed past him to finish the job.

Rachel grinned. Was Zane a good reason to stay? He was certainly different to the Wellington crew, people she'd been used to hanging out with for years. She looked away. It wasn't about Zane.

It wasn't until the film crew had piled into a van and gone off looking for a social life, ably led by Jim Connelly, that Rachel went looking for Zane. She knew he hadn't left yet because she could hear the sound of a saw coming from the woods. She'd pleaded a headache and had managed to get everyone else away. She wanted to be alone with Zane.

He was around the back, where the low sun filtered through the trees which edged the property, finishing tidying up in the garden. It was hot up here and he'd taken off his t-shirt and had tucked it in his worn shorts—shorts that had definitely seen better days, thank God. Her eyes lingered there, as he cleaned the blade of the saw with an old cloth. Sweat glistened on his body, highlighting the broad shoulders, and muscled chest and stomach. She wanted to smooth her fingers along his sweaty chest and lick it, taste its saltiness and maleness. A warning bell rang inside her. This was madness. Finally she'd found someone who respected her, who treated her like an individual, not someone literally and figuratively to be screwed, and all she could think about was having sex with him? And, not only that, she wanted to use him to find her daughter. The conflicting thoughts made her head explode. She should leave. But, before she could, he looked up and caught her gaze and she knew there was no going back now.

He put down the saw, smoothed his hands over his shorts and walked toward her, seemingly unaware of his lack of decent clothes.

"Rachel," he said with that super sexy voice of his, as if he were purring her name in her ear. A tingle flowed through her before coming to rest somewhere low inside, where it nestled like an impatient fledgling, creating havoc in her gut and lower.

"Zane." She stepped forward out from the darkness of the trees into the golden light of the garden and held out a tray.

"Drink?"

"Water, thanks," said Zane, dusting off the sawdust. "It's been some day off!"

She passed him a glass of water. "You've been brilliant. I don't know what we'd have done without you."

"Nothing, I suspect." He drank the whole glass and her gaze was fixed on his throat. He replaced it on the tray. "Apart from you, of course. All the others seemed to hang around, watching."

She shrugged. "That *is*, actually, their job."

"Well, they did nothing very well." He grinned. "I don't know how you put up with it all." He shook his head. "It's a weird world."

She frowned and poured herself another glass of Champagne. She sipped her wine. "It's *my* world," she said quietly. "It might appear a bit over the top to you, but it's not really. It's only a bit of acting for the cameras. If I didn't, it'd make one hell of a boring show." She shook her hair back as she thought about the show.

"You see," said Zane thoughtfully. She looked up. "There you go. With that flippy thing you do with your hair. You do that on TV."

She clamped her hand to her hair and then smoothed it down. "I didn't know I did."

"I know you don't. It must be something you do for an audience. But there's only me here now. I'm not one of those men from your past who liked you because of your persona. I like the *real* you, not the manufactured you."

Rachel opened her mouth to speak but no words came out. She swallowed and he stepped toward her and pushed her hair back from her face. "There, like that."

Whatever he'd done at that moment would have been right.

He narrowed his eyes. "Let's get out of here."

He held out his hand and she took it and they walked around the corner of the deck, down the steps and out onto the lawn which fell away into the sandy beach. "Where are we going?"

"Fancy a walk?"

"Sure."

"Good," he said. "I want to show you something."

They walked along the drive and out, onto the road. A little way along, Zane opened a gate in a field, down one side of which a pathway ran up the hill. With a rush of excitement, Rachel suddenly she knew where she was being led. At the top of the path, on the summit of the hill, they looked down.

Across the bay the other arm of the harbor caught the last of the sunlight, before it dipped behind the hills. The tide was out and the mudflats where the river ran into the harbor were golden. Before her was Belendroit, peeping from behind the trees, its many lanterns—lit even during the day— a family tradition her mother had insisted on continuing. *So my family can always find their way home*, her mother had said. Seemed it was working—for her, for now at least.

"It's beautiful, isn't it?" said Zane, looking out.

She followed his gaze, seeing its beauty but not truly feeling it, not like she used to, so many years ago.

She shrugged. "Yes, it is."

He looked at her strangely, as if sensing her appreciation was only superficial. "You don't sound convinced."

She shrugged again. "Sometimes it's hard to disassociate a place with what you felt here."

"And what you felt was bad?"

She shrugged. "Sad, more like." She drew in a deep breath. "But hopefully not for much longer."

It wasn't until he kissed her that she realized he'd thought she was referring to him. She should tell him the truth about why she'd returned to Akaroa. She should tell him that the lurch of excitement she'd felt when she realized he was taking her to the marae was all to do with the fact that he might lead her to her daughter.

He took her hand. "Come on, there's some people I want you to meet."

Suddenly Rachel was scared. What if Zane's grandmother blurted out the truth about her past, warned Zane away, and prevented her from finding her daughter? After all, she'd made it totally clear all those years ago that the child would have nothing to do with the Connelly family, just as both sides of the family had wanted.

Zane grinned, obviously imagining her reluctance to be shyness. "Okay. Let's keep it to us today. I'll take you back to my place and we can have a beer. Besides, the main person I want to introduce you to isn't there. Gran's away at a neighboring marae which means half the kids are too."

Relieved, she nodded. "How come you have a different surname to your gran?"

"Black was my step-father's surname. He wasn't married to my mother for long, although long enough for us to form a bond and for him to adopt me, but he was a good man and helped me out of a bad situation. It was through his influence that I got into a good boarding school. He died trying to settle a dispute between gangs. I kept his name out of respect."

"And your birth father didn't mind?"

"Not so much. He had his hands full with my step-mother, here at the marae, and all the children they had."

Including Tommy, thought Rachel. The father of her child.

"But you didn't want to stay in Auckland."

"No. This is my home. I'll show you."

They turned their backs to the harbor and walked along

the ridge to the next valley toward the marae, and the cluster of houses which were on Maori land, where Zane lived.

"I'm sorry about the whole scene down there with Sean. He's… well, he's used to doing things like that. I mean he's a great camerman but…"

"But he's a…" There was a pause when all the words which Zane had every right to call Sean floated between them. "He's not a very nice man."

Rachel grinned. She knew exactly what he was going to say, but Zane being Zane wasn't about to say such things in front of a woman. "Exactly. In fact, I've heard people say a lot worse things about him than that."

"And I'm sure they're accurate." His eyes searched her face as if trying to make his mind up about something.

He reached forward and plucked a small twig from her hair. "Looks like I didn't clear the garden very well."

"Why are you doing all this anyway? I mean, don't get me wrong, Dad's appreciative and accepts your offers of help in a way he never does with us. And not in the way Sean does, either."

Zane huffed a brief laugh. "I like your Dad. We get along."

"Yeah. With you, he's not crazy competitive, he's quieter somehow."

"That's because you lot are all like him. You need some Maori blood in you to make you chill a bit."

"You're hardly chill. You never stop working."

He shrugged. "That's different and you know it. I'm not talking about being busy, or being productive, I'm talking about working yourselves up into stupid whirlwinds of ego and competition. None of that's worth it."

"How do you know?"

"Because that's what I used to do, darlin'." He stepped closer and brushed his knuckles lightly over her cheek, pushing her hair back from her face in the process. "So, would you like a beer with me on the porch?"

She smiled in agreement, unable to do anything else because her whole body still lingered on the sensation which his fingers had created on her skin. It skittered down and caused the fledglings in her stomach to get over-excited again.

"My house is over there." He indicated a house which stood apart from the others. His house was one of the older ones, late nineteenth-century she'd have guessed, but looked like it was in the process of being renovated. It must have been one of the original homesteads because it appeared pretty grand on the outside.

"It's beautiful."

"It's old, is what it is. But it *will* be beautiful when I'm finished with it."

Beyond it was the marae, outside of which a cluster of kids played and she could hear a band practising inside. A group of elderly people sat around a table sharing a beer and a laugh.

Rachel searched the kids, stopping on each one, trying to see if there was anyone who was around the age of her daughter. "Any of your nieces and nephews here?"

He laughed. "They're *all* my nieces and nephews, irrespective of their parentage. I feel responsible for them all."

He took her hand and they walked across the grass to the rear of his property. A hand-made wooden bench sat next to an old sofa which was on a totally different scale to the old sofas at Belendroit. This sofa sagged, its springs were falling out, and one side was held up by bricks.

Rachel sat on the wooden bench which was sturdily made and softened with bright cushions. The view looked out across the valley, away from the marae toward the sea, with the trees coming close to one side, overhanging the veranda.

"This is lovely."

"Yeah. When I came back here, there were a few houses that were empty and I decided on this one straight away. It was a wreck with a view. I could do something about the wreck part."

"But you didn't have to do anything about the view." She looked around at the books, the magazines and a laptop whose cable went through the window inside. "I bet you spend most of your time out here."

He grinned and handed her a beer from the fridge which was also outside, sheltered from the elements in a corner of the veranda. "Yep. I never could stand feeling hemmed in."

"So you don't miss your old life?"

He leaned against the balustrade of the old veranda which was partially re-built. Standing in front of her, with the view behind him and his hips at eye level, Rachel reckoned she had the best view.

He was silent and looked away. Rachel frowned. Her question hadn't really meant anything. She would have bet anything that he'd have answered with an immediate 'no'.

"You do," she said. He caught her gaze and his expression was different to normal. There was a sadness there she hadn't seen before. "I'm surprised. I thought you were happy."

"Sure, I'm happy. But do I miss the old life? Of course I do. They were the best of times. I was an All Black—it's an ambition for any Kiwi kid. And I was damn good one."

Rachel's eyes widened in surprise at the swear word. It was the first time she'd heard him swear, albeit it mildly.

"But isn't there any way you could still be a part of that world?"

He looked at her steadily as he took a swig of beer. "You don't understand, Rachel. I have no interest in the 'world' of rugby. Only in playing. You can't imagine what it's like to catch a loose ball, turn things around and run up the field, your heart pounding, watching and sensing where the opposition would try to tackle you, avoid them with a few choice steps, see the line ahead, make the decision, try for the line or pass it on. It's like every part of you is working together, at the peak of performance—your brain, your body, and not least, your instincts…" He exhaled heavily and looked away. "It's magic." He pursed his lips together and shook his head and took another swig of beer and looked directly at her again. "And I miss it every day of my life." His voice was the usual sexy, deep, soft voice, but this time it held a hollowness and bleakness which seeped into her.

"I'm so sorry, Zane. I had no idea."

He shrugged lightly. "It's okay. That's life." He stamped his foot. "My knee's fixed and good for everyday use, just can't risk it anymore for extreme use. I tried and they can't patch it up anymore."

She glanced down at the knee. It looked so strong and solid she couldn't imagine it wasn't working in top condition.

"Are you hungry? There's a hangi steaming which they'll be opening up soon."

"Thanks, but no. I've done enough tasting today." She rose. "Besides I should get back to prepare for tomorrow's session."

"Let me walk you home," he said, slipping his hand into hers.

"No, thanks."

He frowned. "There are no street lights down the hill. I'll walk you. I know the path like the back of my hand."

She pressed her hand against his chest, trying to focus on what she was about to say, rather than the heat emanating from his body, rather than the hairs that tickled the palm of her hand.

"No," she repeated and stepped a little closer. She looked up into his eyes. "No."

He drew in a sharp intake of breath and tugged her toward him. She came hard into contact with his body. She spread her fingers over his bare chest, the dark nipples, the firm strong muscles of a natural athlete, not bulked up unnaturally by a gym.

He tilted her chin up and his eyes roved over her face. He thrust his fingers through her hair and held her face steady. Slowly he lowered his lips to hers and kissed her. His lips weren't as soft as they looked as they pressed against hers. For all his gentleness, this big man was holding back and as soon as he felt the small gasp against his mouth, the kiss intensified. He put both hands around her back, feeling carefully at first and then holding her tight as if he never wanted to let her go.

She gasped as his tongue slid along her lips and parted her mouth, and met hers with a caress that turned her weak at the knees. From gentle arousal to raging need, her libido roared into life as she slid her hands up around his naked chest and back, fingering, gripping and stroking the dips and contours of his muscled body.

Suddenly he gripped her hands and pulled them straight down, and pulled away from the kiss. They stood, foreheads pressed, panting with desire.

"Are you sure?" he asked.

"Yes, of course. Why? Aren't you?"

"I don't do one night stands, Rachel. Especially with someone like you."

"Someone like me? What do you mean?"

"Someone who could break my heart."

She swallowed, blown away by the thought that she could do such a thing. It had always been the other way around.

"I wouldn't break your heart."

"Are you sure about that? Think about it. Believe me, I'd love nothing better than to carry you inside and make love to you." Rachel shivered with desire and looked up hopefully because she as sure as hell would like nothing better, too. But his expression was firm. "But I won't, not unless you can see a future for us. I've had years of fooling around with no thought to the future, but that kind of life didn't bring me happiness. Maybe a short-lived kind, but it only left me hungry for more."

"Like eating food stuffed with calories and no goodness?"

He grinned. "Exactly. Like fast food. Don't get me wrong, I wolf it back given the chance, but it doesn't last the distance. And"—he touched her cheek gently—"I really want to last the distance with you."

"Wolfing me back sounds pretty attractive at the moment," Rachel said with a rueful grin. But even while she spoke she thought of the secret she was withholding from him. It wasn't fair on either of them to take this to a different level until he knew the truth. Something of her thoughts must have filtered through to her expression, because he nodded and stepped away.

"I'll walk you home and you think about what I've said. And, if you're still interested, there will be plenty of time for binge eating."

They went inside and he switched on a small lamp in the hallway by a window and it shone out, down the steps and into the garden. She didn't go inside but watched him, each movement of his powerful body deliberate and controlled. She let the cooler night breeze try to calm down her arousal, although she really only saw one way to deal with it —and that was to satisfy it. But that didn't look to be happening any time soon. Unless... unless she agreed to have a serious relationship with him. And how could she? Because at some point her secret would be revealed and that would be an end to it all. He'd have no further interest in her.

She greeted his smile with one of her own as he pulled on a shirt, coming out the house.

"Don't you lock it?"

"No." He grinned. "If anyone other than family tried to enter here they'd been given short shrift by the others."

"So your family come and go as they like?"

"Sure. That's why I keep the fridge fully stocked. Some of the family don't have much money. They return to the marae when their own families have enough of them." He suddenly looked fierce. "Anyway, if they're hungry they know they can always have a feed here… a good life here."

She'd been right. He'd protect his family with his life. He *was* protecting them with his life, whether they knew it or not.

They walked side by side to the top of the hill and looked over the harbor, down at the lights of Belendroit and, farther along the harbor, Akaroa. It was beautiful… too perfect a view to be real. She suddenly had a deep need to be alone, to consider her own imperfect future. "Goodnight, Zane."

He frowned. "Are you sure?"

"Sure, I'm sure." She indicated Belendroit. "I'm almost there."

"If that's what you want…"

She nodded. "It is. Goodnight."

"Goodnight, Rachel. I'll see you around, yes?"

"Sure." And he would. Not because she saw a future with him—family came first and he'd hate her when he discovered that she and her family had given her child up for adoption. But because the need to find her child was too strong and Zane was her best bet for finding her daughter.

7

*T*urned out their new relationship wasn't so much slow as stationary. Between the filming at Belendroit and Zane's work on the tribal council, which was taking him all over the South Island, over a week had passed without Rachel so much as setting eyes on him.

Rachel wandered over to the window for the hundredth time, wondering if she'd see Zane's car in the drive. He said he might come direct from the airport. But the only cars belonged to her father—his ancient, prized Daimler—and the film crew, bumper to bumper along the drive.

She fingered her cellphone in her pocket. He'd rung during his absence, but only late at night, after he'd finished work. During those phone calls he'd told her about the kind of work he and his Maori Board did—about protecting and investing the assets which had been granted them by the Waitangi Tribunal which made them the wealthiest tribe in New Zealand and, more important to Zane's heart, protecting the culture and families of the tribe. She'd listened with a heavy heart as he described the issues facing his people, issues he'd faced as a youngster. She felt his need, she felt his compassion and she also felt, quite viscerally, his anger. Because it was an anger she feared might be directed at her once he found out his niece was also her daughter.

"Rachel!" called the producer.

Rachel jumped around. There were people everywhere, her father in the midst of them all, entertaining and hindering the team by turns. "Yes?"

"Can you finish these photos off here and then we'll get back to shooting the last sequence."

"Sure." The photos were to be included in the new book which accompanied the series. But as she slid a crème caramel under the grill to brown, her phone buzzed. She automatically checked the screen. She sighed. It wasn't Zane. Only a text from her friend, Lucia, who lived on her husband's family estate near Wellington, inviting her to stay the weekend. She smiled at Lucia's excitement about a weekend party she was arranging with the Mackenzie clan. Rachel's sister, Lizzi, and her family would be there, being close friends of Callum and Gemma Mackenzie. She was tempted. She adored Lucia and Guy's long-awaited-for twins. But, she tapped the phone against her lips, she was torn. There was a lot of unfinished business around here, in more ways than one.

"Rachel!" said the photographer, frowning at her as if she'd gone mad. "You've described it as golden in the book. That"—he waved his camera lens at the offending dessert— "is more like burnt."

"Damn!" Rachel put on the oven glove and grabbed the dessert from under the grill and slid it onto the wooden board. She wafted the smoke away with her hand, feeling flustered. "It's okay. I made a backup." She slid the new one under the grill and gave herself a talking to. She *had* to focus. She suddenly had a vision of herself performing the circus trick of spinning plates on the top of long poles. She imagined herself moving around constantly, making sure the poles gyrated enough to keep the plates from falling. The TV series, the accompanying book, her father, Zane, and not least, her child. She had a horrible feeling that if she took her mind of any of the things that mattered to her, they could all come tumbling down.

~

IT WAS the last day of the board meeting and Zane was relieved. Chairing the group wasn't his idea of fun but his reputation for good judgement and the *mana* associated with his past sporting achievements had lumbered him with the role of Chairperson, not only of his sub-tribe, but also of the main tribe which covered over two-thirds of the South Island. And his strong sense of duty and responsibility, inherited from his grandmother, made him unable to reject the position, even if he would rather be out with the kids, kicking a rugby ball around.

As he walked into the boardroom of their new corporate headquarters in Christchurch, everyone greeted him. His tribe had always been under pressure—in past centuries from immigrants and the government—and now, from the issues which plagued all lower socio-economic groups—unemployment, drugs and gangs, not to mention the need to keep his culture and language alive. It was a constant battle over resources and political maneuvering.

He looked around at his board—some old, steeped in traditional ways, and some young and reactionary, wanting to blast away the links that kept them anchored to the past and move them into the future, using all their valuable assets. It was down to Zane to lead them all, sticking firmly to his principles, which made his decisions easier to make, even while they made his life more difficult.

The first day had been especially testing but the meeting was at last concluding with family business around adoptions and family access. It was always a sensitive area and one that tested Zane's love of family against his protective instinct.

"And finally, we've had a request regarding one of our *whangai* children." The man looked over his glasses at Zane. "One of your family, Zane. We wouldn't normally raise this at board level but this is an unusual situation and we need to clarify some principles. As you know, Maori informal adoption occupies a legal gray area."

Zane wondered which of his large extended family the man could be referring to.

"The child involved is a"—the man referred to his notes— "Henrietta Tau."

"Etta?" Zane sat back with surprise. Etta lived on his marae and went to the local school where he worked. He kept an eye on her, just as he did his other nieces and nephews because Etta was his brother's child. "Who wants to know about her?"

"Her mother, apparently"

Zane felt a flash of indignation and anger. "Her *mother*? Her mother who didn't want her at her birth and who gave away her own child to my brother's family when it didn't suit her to raise the child herself? *That* person?"

The man shrugged. "She was quite young at the time." He flipped through the pages. "Her name isn't available. Looks like they hushed the whole thing up and your family took responsibility."

Zane frowned. He hadn't ever investigated his family's informal adoption of Etta which had happened while he'd been away. He'd had no interest in discovering the identity of the woman who'd abandoned her child. "The usual principles and rules apply. The mother doesn't gain access. It'll disturb the girl. She's settled at school. She's my niece, she lives on the marae, and she's doing well."

The man pushed another piece of paper across the desk. "That fits with a report from one of our counsellors. She suggests that this information remain confidential. The circumstances are unusual—apparently the mother has a high international profile—and the counsellor is concerned about this influence on Etta, who apparently is quite head-strong. Therefore, she concluded that it wasn't in the best interests of Henrietta—Etta—to become known to her mother."

Zane scanned through the report, noting the name of the counsellor, someone with the same firm ideas about adoption as his own. "Then the case is clear."

"But apparently the woman is a public figure. She could make trouble."

"That's irrelevant and has no bearing on the matter. If she applies for access under the Guardianship Act, then we'll face that later." The fact that the woman had a high profile simply made things worse in his mind. How dare she return demanding to find out about the child who she'd happily given away ten years before? "The principles are clear. And there don't appear to be any extenuating circumstances, nothing to change our mind, so deny the application." Zane grimly flicked over the page and looked down determinedly at the next item of business. But, as the man's voice fell into a droning, tired monologue about a local land issue, Zane's mind clung to the anger which the previous business had roused.

Thirty years before, his young mother had left him on Ti Tahi Marae, giving him up for informal adoption. But then she'd turned up and his memory of that day remained firmly in his mind. He'd been around Etta's age. His world had shifted on its axis when she'd come back and took him away from his home on the marae at Akaroa, to Auckland, to a world of concrete and passing strangers. But he'd been lucky for a while. His mother had been briefly re-married to a good man—named Black—who'd helped Zane move on when he needed to, concerned that, like so many of the young people, he'd resort to gangs for a family. So his step-father had helped Zane get into a boarding school for Maori boys and Zane had thrived. He'd focused on his studies and rugby and left his birth mother's world far behind. Zane had kept the name Black to honor his step-father and, after he'd been launched into the elite rugby world, Zane Black he'd stayed.

The whole experience had left him with a desire to protect children, to give the best experience he could to them and, in order to do that, he needed to save them from the love of people who, simply by virtue of their birth, felt they had a claim on a person. Zane believed they'd lost that claim when the decision had been made to give their child away. Some people described him as uncompromising, others as black and white. If Zane had to describe himself he'd call himself principled. There was only ever one right answer.

RACHEL HAD TAKEN advantage of some technical difficulties with filming to escape into Akaroa. She'd left behind the cameraman berating the distance they were from Wellington and the delay it would take to get the required parts. He blamed production, who blamed the technical department in Wellington. Rachel left them blaming each other, tempers flaring, and her father happily trying to provide distraction with anecdotes and wine. One last glance at the unhappy group showed that the wine was proving the most successful tactic.

She walked along the beach road to Akaroa enjoying the fresh air. It felt like an age since she'd been outside during the day. She'd forgotten that *that* was what her life had been like in Wellington—inside all the time—whether inside a hot kitchen, a hot studio, or a hot stuffy evening venue, she was always hemmed in. Not that she'd seen it that way. But now she could hardly believe she'd put up with it for so long.

She stopped on the outskirts of Akaroa and looked around at the row of colonial houses, with their white-painted fretwork and balconies overlooking the harbor which was demure and gray under a heated cloudy sky. People were enjoying late lunches in the café at the end of the short pier, and boats bobbed alongside, waiting for the busy weekend ahead when the small town would welcome visitors, from New Zealand and overseas.

Rachel had always been irritated by visitors when she was growing up. But now she enjoyed the variety they added to the place. If she didn't watch herself, she'd find herself thinking of Akaroa as home again.

Instead of going directly into the café, Rachel was about to walk past the school when a car hooted and drew up on the other side of the road. It was Zane. He lowered his sunglasses as he caught her gaze, and smiled, a heart-stopping, too rare smile. She waved and walked across the road toward him.

"Ms Connelly!" he called, switching off the engine and jumping out the car.

She grinned. "Mr. Black! Fancy seeing you here. I thought you had one more night in Christchurch."

He put his arm around her and kissed her chastely on the cheek. "I'd had enough. Another evening, surrounded by men talking politics and finance, would have done my head in."

"Their loss, my gain."

He raised an eyebrow. "I'd hoped you'd think that." He

licked his lips and drew back his bottom lip with his teeth. The glint in his eyes couldn't be described in any other way except naughty. "Busy?"

"As it happens… no. Technical glitches with filming have given me the afternoon off. And I can make that evening, too, if it suits."

He nodded slowly as his quick gaze took her in from head to toe. "It suits."

She blushed at the intimate way his gaze lingered on her body. "You're looking very smart," she said, deciding a change in subject was the wisest course of action. "I haven't seen you in a suit before." She cocked her head to one side, assessing the silk lining of his jacket, the classic fit of the shirt, the silk tie hanging loose, and the perfect fit of the pants. Very perfect. "European styling, designed to impress."

"If it's impressed you, it's done its job."

"I didn't say that. I simply recognize clothing that's designed to impress."

"Yeah, I guess. It's a legacy of my days as an All Black. An Italian designer gave me suits in exchange for some modeling."

She nearly choked on a laugh. "You? A model? I can't imagine that."

"What? You think I'm not pretty enough?" He grinned, rolling back on his shiny leather-soled shoes.

"I wouldn't describe you as 'pretty', exactly."

"Good."

"But I can see exactly why your services as a model would be required."

"Is that right? And why's that?"

She stepped closer to him, only the bag she was holding between the two of them, oblivious to anyone else around them. "Buy me a drink"—she indicated the café at the end of the pier—"and I might tell you."

His eyes grew dark before he shook his head. "The things I have to do to earn compliments."

"Oh, I didn't say anything about compliments."

He threw his head back and laughed. "You have me intrigued now, Ms Connelly." He locked his car and offered Rachel his arm. "Shall we?"

Rachel couldn't figure out what was different about walking arm in arm with Zane. She enjoyed the company of men, loved flirting and dating, yet she'd never felt like this before. A range of words and descriptions flitted through her mind as they walked along the pier, the slick water flowing beneath the wooden boards. But she settled on 'girlish'. She felt as if ten years had been rolled back and she was a teenager again. Except a little wiser and a whole lot more sexually aware.

They were immediately shown to a table which hadn't been there minutes earlier. The maitre d' fussed over them, snapping his fingers for a waitress to appear out of nowhere with a carafe of water and glasses in hand, as he welcomed them and set them a place by the waterside.

Zane glanced at the back of the maitre d' as he walked away, leaving them alone. "Do you have this effect every time you go out to eat?"

Rachel placed her elbows on the table and rested her chin on her steepled fingers. "Everywhere except places run by my own sisters. They make no concession to me, I can assure you!"

"Ah, that makes sense. There's no one like family to bring you back down to earth."

"Are you suggesting I'm not a down-to-earth kind of girl?"

He threw up his hands in surrender. "I guess I am." He leaned forward, echoing her stance. "And you know what? I wouldn't have it any other way." He bridged the inches of space between their hands and brushed his finger along hers. "I've missed you."

Something strange happened to her stomach—a flip, a surge of desire—which made her lick her lips and look at his own. She answered the touch of his finger by moving her forefinger over the tip of his strong square fingernail and around the pad beneath. As her finger drew toward his palm, he curled his fingers around hers and caressed her with an intimate, and yet innocent action, which only intensified her desire for him.

"I have you, now. You can't escape." He was joking but there was something in his eyes and in the curve of those sensuous lips which told her the truth. He wasn't joking. He wanted her and he wanted to keep hold of her.

"Maybe I don't want to escape." She wasn't joking either.

The waiter cleared his throat and they both looked round. With a smile at Zane, Rachel slid her finger from his grip. It slid easily. He had no need to hold on tight, and, she guessed, he'd never try. Women would come willingly to him, and willingly stay. She liked that.

"How about you order for us, Rachel," said Zane, closing the menu.

"Sure." She glanced at the menu, and ordered something quick and easy for them both. She didn't want a protracted lunch and, from the look in Zane's eyes, he was in complete agreement.

"Thank you." She smiled at the waiter who grinned back.

Zane watched the interaction. "You're lovely with people, you know that?"

"Aren't most people?"

"No, they're not. Especially when they're famous. People tend to forget about other people then. Perhaps that's why I didn't imagine, when I first met you, that you *were* famous."

"It could also be something to do with the fact you rarely watch TV and have zero interest in gossip."

"It's not only that. Fame usually brings out the worst in people. But, for some reason, not with you. Or, maybe I'm wrong. Maybe it does."

"How so?"

"Maybe your worst is better than most people's best."

"Now you're making fun of me."

His face suddenly went serious. "No, I'm not. I really like you, Rachel. More than like. I respect you."

He sat back in his chair and took a sip of water, waiting for her to reply. She didn't know what response to give. She felt his compliment more deeply than any of her exes proclaiming undying lust for her. "Respect... is good," she said at last. Respect, she thought, might also be strong enough to weather the storm which would ensue after her secret had been revealed.

"It's a good basis to work forward from."

"And you want to work forward? With me?"

"Yes. Most definitely. How do you feel? I mean, I know you've had a rough time in the past with men and coming down here was one way to get away from all of that." He paused, waiting for her to speak, but she was too charmed by his sensitivity. "And..." He took a deep breath. "I understand that you might not want to begin a relationship." Another pause and his eyes narrowed this time. "Rachel," he warned. "Don't keep me in suspense."

She warred with herself. How could she resist this man? And yet he was right, on more levels than he knew. "Honestly? I don't know. Life's complicated."

"It can always be simplified."

"Not easily."

"Why? Is there someone in Wellington?"

"No, there's no one in Wellington."

"Then, what is it?"

She should tell him now. Tell him about her child. Tell him that she suspected he would know her daughter, at least know *of* her, and where Rachel could find her. But the words tied up in an almighty knot in her head and the moment passed. It might be all right, she said to herself. He'd said he respected her. It might be enough.

"No," said Zane. "Don't tell me. It's your business. Now"— he looked up as their meals were placed before them—"let's eat."

Zane continued to talk, to fill the silence, and slowly the knot of anxiety over her secret—the secret she would tell Zane, but later—unwound. Zane kept the conversation light and flirtatious and an hour passed easily and enjoyably. It wasn't until the dessert menu was presented that things hotted up again.

She glanced at Zane over the top of the menu and caught his gaze. "What do you fancy?"

All she could see were his eyes, which crinkled at the corner at her question. And one raised eyebrow. She cleared her throat, not waiting for his answer. "I hear the sorbet is wonderful here."

Zane glanced at the menu, closed it and placed it on the table and leaned over to her. "What I want is something wonderful that will melt in my mouth."

Rachel really hadn't imagined he could say anything that would turn her on further. But it seemed he could. She sat back and grabbed the menu and fanned her face. "Zane!" She shot him a warning glance. "Don't do this to me."

"Do what?" he asked in mock innocence. He took a sip of water and Rachel could see he was as aroused as she was.

"You know exactly what."

He licked his lips and Rachel couldn't take her eyes off them, as she imagined parts of her melting under his tongue.

He slipped his foot alongside hers. The heat of his body traveled up her legs. She groaned. "Zane," she warned. He pressed his leg against hers. "If you do that, I can't guarantee I won't leap across this table and climb into your arms."

His leg stayed as he digested the thought. He pressed his leg closer. "I'd kind of like to see that."

"Oh no, you wouldn't! I really don't believe you'd appreciate images of me and you going viral on the internet." She indicated a nearby table where both occupants were busy with their cell phones. "They could take a photo and upload it to Instagram without us even knowing."

He sighed and pulled away his leg from hers. He sat back on the chair and his face relaxed into a smile. He'd rolled his white shirt sleeves up and the sea breeze ruffled his hair which had grown a shade too long. It was all she could do to not walk over and sit in his lap and kiss him, even after all she'd said.

"Tell me what you're thinking," he asked.

"I'm thinking... that..." She thought better of revealing her thoughts. "That I can't decide between the ice-cream and the sorbet."

"You want something to cool you down?"

"I think so."

"Um," he said. "Come to think of it, I have some ice-cream in the freezer at home. Care to try out my culinary genius at home?"

It was exactly what she cared to do. "That would be nice."

"Good. I have to drop by the school first, and then I'll take you back to my place and woo you further with creamy New Zealand ice cream, straight from the supermarket."

"Wonderful," she murmured, her mind not on the ice cream.

"But, I have to say, I kind of like you hot and bothered."

. . .

WATCHING Rachel's breasts heave as he brushed his knee inside hers, had Zane even more eager to leave. Okay, he might have wanted to take his time getting to know Rachel, make sure she was as interested as he was, but a week without her was quite enough. Seeing her so relaxed, so beautiful and so damn sexy, had him anxious to get her home with him. Alone, for once. But he had to pick up some papers he needed to grade before school on Monday.

He paid the bill and, his arm around her shoulders, they walked back to the car. He didn't care who saw, only that they knew that he was with her. He felt possessive for once. She got into the car and he was immediately aware of her fragrance. He took a deep breath and let his gaze slip to her legs where her dress had ridden up. Slim, tanned. He could almost feel her as if his hand were sliding up...

She locked in the seatbelt and looked at him with a smile as if knowing what thoughts had passed through his mind. And not only knew them, but acknowledged her mind was tending the same way. He hoped not, otherwise they'd be making love in the car, at the side of a busy street.

He cleared his throat. "I'll make it a brief stop at the school."

A few minutes later, he parked the car outside the school, glanced around to make sure there were no stray cell phones pointing their way, and gave her a long, lingering kiss. She groaned with a need which he was only too aware of himself. "I won't be long."

RACHEL WATCHED him walk quickly across to the administration block. It was hot in the car so she stepped out and wandered inside the school grounds. It was recess and all the kids were playing in the yard and out in the adjacent field. She sat on a bench and looked around. Any of these kids could be hers. Any one of them. Her eyes lingered on one girl bossily telling a group how to do something. She smiled. Except for the blonde curly hair, she could have been her daughter.

Then her eyes moved on to a girl sitting quietly in the corner reading, twiddling her plait as she did so. She had thick dark hair and when she glanced up nervously, her eyes were wide and large, like Rachel's. But if Rachel had spent more time on her books instead of having fun, she'd never have got herself pregnant in the first place.

Then she heard a shout and saw Zane, hands on hips, looking across the playground toward the playing fields. She followed his gaze, curious to see who he was telling off. It didn't take her long to figure it out. At the top of the cross bar of a rugby goalpost, a girl was holding her hands steadily out either side as if she were a ballerina and walking along it as if it were a tight rope. Rachel gasped. It was at least three meters off the ground and the girl didn't wear any shoes, only shorts and a t-shirt revealing a skinny, but very determined, figure.

She didn't look right or left, but stared levelly ahead at the opposite goalpost. Below her a group of boys chanted and clapped, counting each step she made. One of them jeered. "You can't do it!" They were soon scattered by the approach of Zane. One look at him and they fell back, looking sheepish. He didn't need to say a word.

For one tense moment, she wondered what Zane would do. But he didn't call out again. He'd only done that when he saw what she'd intended to do. If he called out again, it might disturb her concentration which could be worse for her.

The seconds dragged out and still she continued along the cross bar. Finally she made it, and reached out in a leisurely way for the upright, as if she'd never been in any doubt she could do it. She looked around for the boys, her

SOPHIE HAYDON

expression confident and arrogant. "See! You losers! I—"
Whatever else she was about to say was swallowed up by the
sight of Zane glaring up at her.

"Etta! Get down here at once. How many times do I have
to tell you that goal posts are for kicking into, not clambering over."

"I'm not clambering—"

"And don't answer back. Down! Now!"

She bit her lip and sat down on the bar, and then gripped
it either side, flipped upside down and swung down, landing
on the soft turf like an acrobat. She walked up to him with
her head held high.

She performed the whole movement with such skill and
grace that, even from this distance, Rachel could see that
Zane was trying hard not to smile. The girl was evidently a
favorite of his.

As he started talking to her, she looked around and
Rachel caught sight of her profile. She was going to be a
stunner, thought Rachel, with her lustrous dark hair and fine
bone structure. Skinny now, she'd no doubt develop into a
fuller figure, just as she had. Suddenly a chill wave washed
over Rachel. She repeated her thoughts. *Just as she had.*

She was still staring as the girl walked sullenly away
toward the boys before the walk turned into a run and she
punched the air. Zane noticed and shook his head, unable to
prevent the smile now as he returned to Rachel.

"That girl!" he said as he walked out the school grounds.
Before Rachel got in the car she looked back to see the girl
now playing rugby with the boys.

"Who is she?"

"Just one of the kids. A real tomboy. She'd rather be
playing rugby, risking life and limb, than studying. But she's
bright enough. She has her heart set on a rugby scholarship

in the States. With her determination, she could do it, too. Trouble is, she has no sense of self-preservation."

"Who has, at that age?"

"Me. I did," said Zane as they drove off.

"What's her name?"

Zane glanced over his shoulder to make sure it was safe to pull out into the road. "Sorry?" he asked.

"Her name. I just wondered who she was."

"Etta. She lives on the marae. She's part of the whanau."

"She's your niece?"

He gave her a curious glance. "Good guess, although I've so many, I suppose it wasn't that wild a guess."

"No," said Rachel, gazing back at the girl who was running full pelt at a defender, with the rugby ball tucked under her arm. "It wasn't."

"Yeah, my younger half-brother's daughter—Tommy's girl."

Tommy's girl… and hers.

8

"Zane, look, I'm sorry, I'm wanted back at Belendroit."

He frowned but immediately responded by taking a road which would take them back there. "This is sudden. Has something happened?"

"Yeah. I..." She tapped her phone on her knee. "I received a text. I'm needed for a meeting."

He stopped at the junction and glanced at her. She looked the other way, out the window at the shops where people still lingered.

"On a Friday evening," he said. "Unusual."

"My whole life's unusual."

She felt his curious glance burn into the back of her head as she stared at the passing shops, which turned into houses, which turned into countryside. Minutes passed and she didn't speak.

He pulled into the driveway and switched off the engine. He pushed a stray strand of hair off her face. "So... will I see you tomorrow?"

She bit her lip. "Work."

His frowned. "Well, how about next week?"

"I've some meetings scheduled for Wellington." At least that was the truth. But it didn't sound like it after the feeble excuses earlier.

He withdrew his hand, twisted away from her, and sighed.

"I'm sorry," she said lamely.

"Hmm... Me too."

He opened the car door and she followed suit. To her consternation he followed her out of the car and up to the house. "No, really. It's fine. You've your paper grading to do."

She stopped short of the house, lingering on the veranda. She could hear the others inside, a little worse for her father's generous supply of wine. If Zane came into the house, he'd know it was a ruse, know she'd lied. He shoved his hands in his pockets, looked around in confusion, then put one foot on the step and looked up at her. "What's going on, Rachel?"

She should have known that he'd spot a lie a mile off. She should have known that she couldn't fob him off with half-truths and excuses, like a normal guy—like a guy who couldn't have cared less. Because Zane did care.

"I'm sorry, Zane... "

He took a step back, recoiling almost. "Hey, I don't want to force you into making some kind of excuse. I'd just thought"—he looked around as if for some kind of answer from the woods, then back to her, his face resigned and disappointed—"I just thought we were getting on okay."

"We were. I mean we *are*. But... I'm sorry, I can't see that we have a future together."

"Really? Earlier on today you suggested that we had exactly that. What's happened to change your mind?"

Rachel shivered. The late summer heat had gone from the sun. There was a chill in the air, a change of atmosphere, as autumn approached. "Honestly? I don't believe you'll want to be with me in a little while."

"In a little while? What are you talking about?"

"What I'm trying to say is that I don't think it's me who will be changing my mind."

"You mean, it'll be me. And why would I do that?"

"Because… months ago, I set something in train, something which—" She paused, unable to bear the thought of this man hating her.

"Darling!" Sean, the cameraman appeared from inside the house, obviously tipsy from the wine he'd been drinking. He placed his hands either side of his mouth and turned back to the house. "Rachel's back everyone. And she's brought the gardener!" Rachel grimaced in embarrassment.

"What are you doing here, Rach?" asked Amanda, emerging from the back of the house. "I thought you were gone for the day."

Rachel caught sight of Zane's hurt gaze as the truth hit him—she'd been making excuses not to be with him. He shook his head and without saying anything further, walked back to the car.

"Zane!" she called.

He halted for an instant before continuing on without comment. And she knew, there and then, that she had to tell him. She ran down the steps but he'd outpaced her and was revving up the car by the time she reached him. She banged once on the window but he pulled away without looking at her.

She watched him disappear, but part of her was glad. Because what the hell would she have said to him if he had stopped? Nothing short of the truth would have sufficed. And she had no words to explain the tumult of emotion going through her on the discovery of the identity of her child. Equally she had no words to soften the fact that she'd given her baby away… and not just to anyone, but to Zane's family—people he'd protect with his life. Yes, she had to tell him the truth but she had no idea how.

~

ZANE COULDN'T AVOID GOING AROUND to Belendroit any longer. But one thing he could avoid was seeing Rachel. He knew she'd gone to Wellington and that Jim was alone, which was fine with him. He had no idea what had happened, no clue as to the reason for Rachel's abrupt change of mind of the previous week, despite spending every waking moment obsessed with going over and over the events of that afternoon. Had he gone too far? Had he assumed too much? But the memory of how she'd been with him at the café, and afterwards, was enough to reassure him that Rachel had been as ready to take the next step in their relationship as he'd been. Which left the question, why the hell had she backed off so spectacularly? A question to which he had no answer.

With the file of photos under his arm, Zane walked up to the front door which was open as usual. The radio was turned down, and Jim Connelly emerged from the dark hallway.

"Zane!" Jim opened the door wide and greeted Zane enthusiastically. Zane wondered again why he hadn't noticed the similarity between Jim and Rachel before. Both were born entertainers. "Come in, come in. I'm afraid Rachel isn't here. All we have is all this clutter. More filming, you know. Next week."

Zane did know, he'd heard the gossip, but didn't feel as excited as Jim appeared to be about it. He held up the file. "Jim, I need to see Rachel about something but I missed her before she went to Wellington." He paused but, from Jim's expression, Jim had no idea that Zane and Rachel weren't still the best of friends.

"Oh, that's a shame. She'll be back in a few days."

Zane knew that but wanted this sewn up before she re-appeared. "Look, I wanted to ask her permission to use some of the photos which were taken at the school fundraiser. The publicity officer for the council has asked if they can use them and I have to let them know by this morning. Can I leave them with you for her to sign off? If she could email me a response on her return, that would be great."

Jim waved his hand in the air. "No need to ask, my boy! She's a pro, she's used to photos being taken." He paused. "I assume it's for some kind of promotional deal?"

"Yes, of course."

"Then it will be fine."

Zane hesitated. He really didn't want to force Rachel to contact him if she so obviously didn't want to.

"Really, Zane, it's no problem. I'll let her know you've come around and asked. She's in Wellington. No doubt sorting out the details of the US contract."

Zane's heart plummeted. He'd known it was in the offing but he'd hoped that he'd misunderstood, that somehow she was going to refuse it. But who would? Realistically, who on this planet would refuse a lucrative and career changing opportunity to appear on prime time TV in the US—the biggest consumer of Rachel's merchandise in the world? No one.

"Right." He backed away. "Right," he repeated as he looked around, wishing he'd never come. There'd been no point, no reason on this earth why Rachel, who was, at present, negoti-ating international deals, would worry about him using a few photos for promotional purposes. It was the reason she'd done the thing in the first place, wasn't it? "Right," he said again.

"That's a lot of 'rights'," said Jim, uncharacteristically gently. "Would you like to come in and have a drink?"

Zane forced a smile. "Thanks, Jim. I'll get along now. I only wanted to sort this business out."

"Right. You are and Rachel are…"

"Just business. Yes." He stepped away.

"Hm." Jim rolled back on his heels but kept his gaze on Zane. "She'll be back soon, you know."

Zane was about to leave, but paused and looked up at Jim. "When?" He hadn't meant to ask the question and was immediately annoyed with himself for showing interest.

"Sunday night. Then she has a week's filming."

"And then?"

Jim grimaced. "Not sure what's happening after that."

She wasn't coming back. Why he'd ever thought there was a future for them both was a mystery to him. "Right. See you in a few weeks, Jim. I'll come and finish off the garden after Rachel's gone. The place will be too busy before then."

Zane walked away, aware that Jim hadn't moved from the spot on the top of the veranda. Jim was fond of him, Zane knew that. And it was reciprocated. In Jim, he could appreciate the qualities which Rachel exhibited—the extrovert side, the unashamedly performer side. All the things he couldn't appreciate in a partner. Because that was what he'd hoped Rachel would become.

RACHEL GLANCED up at the rapt audience of teenage girls, some chewing gum, others feeding babies, and yet others filming her on their phones, but all of them watching every move Rachel made. Celebrity had some advantages, Rachel thought. Particularly when it came to snagging the attention of the vulnerable, who needed every bit of knowledge they could glean; particularly when it came to fundraising for those people.

"And then..." Rachel paused as she ladled the vegetarian cassoulet into individual dishes and smiled up at the camera which was filming this segment as part of a documentary to raise awareness and funds for the school. "It's ready to eat." She looked up at the small group of girls, holding their babies, who were watching her every move. "Come and try some."

The teenage mums didn't need asking twice. With their babies either asleep in their car seats or prams, or on their hips, they gathered around the teacher's desk which had doubled as the table for the cooking demonstration and accepted a bowl of cassoulet. Amid growing chatter, murmurs of approval, and squawks from the babies, Rachel stepped back and the teacher approached her. She always enjoyed coming to the school which taught teenage mums, *He Huarahi Tamariki*—A Chance for Children. Apart from the wonderful selflessness of the teaching staff who were constantly trying to raise funds to provide an education for the teenage mothers, the place had a feeling of real joy about it.

"Thanks again for doing this. The girls can't get enough of you." Lauren, the principal of the school, joined the girls in tasting the inexpensive dish, complete with homemade stock, and pulled an appreciative face.

"I love it. I wouldn't miss it for the world. And thanks for agreeing to have the cameras here, too." She gestured toward the two cameramen.

"Are you kidding? The girls would love to appear in your TV series. They can't stop talking about it. Of course they'd prefer it if you combined it with some kind of reality dating game."

Rachel rolled her eyes. "Me and dating don't go. I

wouldn't touch *that* concept with a barge pole. Seriously, I'm happy to help. I love coming here and if there's anything else I can do, let me know."

Lauren hesitated.

Rachel frowned. "Is there something?"

"I didn't know how to ask you. But I wondered if you'd do something on a more personal level."

Rachel's stomach tightened, afraid of what was coming. But she didn't let it show, she was too much of a pro for that. "Like what?"

Lauren's gaze didn't waver. "Tell them your story."

Rachel broke eye contact and moved some empty bowls onto a tray. "Story?" she muttered.

She felt a hand on her arm and she turned to Lauren, someone she'd come to know well over the past five years of her involvement with the school.

"I know it's hard, Rachel. But it would mean a lot to the kids. And I think it could be helpful to you."

"Helpful?" Rachel felt vaguely irritated. She really liked Lauren but she didn't need anyone's pity or understanding. She bristled. "I can't see how."

"You told me what happened to you early on in our friendship, but I doubt you've told many others."

Rachel was torn as to whether to continue the conversation or nip it in the bud. But when Lauren's hand squeezed her arm in a gesture of sympathy the remaining barriers fell. She drew in a deep breath and nodded slowly. "Okay, what do you want me to do?"

THERE WASN'T a dry eye in the classroom as Rachel twisted her hands together in an uncharacteristically unsure movement. "And that was that. I left my baby behind. I walked out and I never saw her again."

"What, never?" asked one of the girls.

"No. Her adoptive family didn't want our involvement. They thought it would be disruptive."

"I'd give them disruptive!" said one girl, sitting back in her chair with a grunt. "I'd go round there and demand to see her and there wouldn't be anything they could do about it. And if they tried anything, I'd get my brother to sort them out. You want to borrow my brother, miss?"

Rachel laughed. "I have four of my own, thank you. But I don't want anyone to sort anything out." She glanced across at the cameraman. "You've stopped filming."

"Yeah," he said. "And I'm going to delete what I have done."

"Sean?"

As the girls were talking, she walked over to Sean who was fiddling with his camera lens and putting things away.

"Sean?" she repeated. "It's not like you to *not* film something like that."

"You mean something private? Something that meant something to you?"

"Yes."

"No, you're right. But, you know, even dumb-asses like me know when something's not right. And it's not right for you to bare your soul to the world. That's private. That's *your* business."

"*My* business," she repeated. "Yes, but maybe it'll help others to know about it."

"You're doing enough, Rachel. You don't have to put yourself out to public scrutiny to help these girls. You've helped them already by telling your story to them. They'll probably tell people, but I won't, and my camera won't."

She squeezed his hand. "I appreciate that, Sean. Although, you know, it's time I moved on and was more open about my past."

He shrugged. "That's your decision. But baby steps, yes? Baby steps."

"Yeah. And I want you to take the film and use it as part of the documentary. Because it's not only about me. It's about sharing my story and maybe, just maybe, helping other kids like I was to move forward."

"Okay." He kissed Rachel on the cheek. "Good on you, Rach."

Not so good, maybe. But perhaps she could change that. And it had to be where it all started… in Akaroa.

And as Rachel walked away, his words repeated in her brain. Baby steps. And her next baby steps would be to return home, back to Akaroa, to Belendroit and to Zane. To explain and, hopefully, to gain some answers.

RACHEL DESULTORILY FLIPPED through the airline's magazine as the Christchurch-bound flight took off from Wellington. It had been an interesting week one way or another. After her initial reluctance to tell the girls at the school about her personal history, Rachel had found the experience liberating. She hoped that by the time the documentary was aired, she'd be in touch with her own daughter, one way or another.

She'd managed to delay her decision about the States for another month. The response to her request for access to the tribal authorities would be available any day now and, once it was, she'd tell Zane. If she had the backing of the authorities, she'd be able to talk it through with Zane from a position of strength. And if she didn't, then she'd talk it through with him anyway, because she'd be investigating her rights under the Guardianship Act. Either way, it wouldn't be easy. Either way, Zane would hate her. She could imagine Zane's expression—cold, distancing, and full of disdain—as his opinion of her plummeted into the gutter. Either way, she had no future with him. And the thought devastated her.

She felt more for him than she had meant to, than she'd wanted to, than she had any right to. But she couldn't avoid the confrontation. Not only because of Etta. But because she was the reason she'd returned to Akaroa in the first place—to face up to her past, to uncover the secrets and weed out the pain and self-hatred she'd planted so many years ago.

She sighed and opened the magazine once more, trying to distract herself from her thoughts of Etta, so tantalizingly close now, and of Zane, a man whose principles ruled his life and therefore ruled *her*, *out* of his life.

Akaroa. The headline focused her immediately. She opened out the double-page spread of publicity material and photos and did a double-take when she saw images of herself dotted across the pages. It was of the fundraiser—her in a raft of situations, with the kids, the mayor, the teachers, cooking. Whoever had written the article was spinning her involvement for all it was worth to raise the profile of the area. And expensive advertisements adorned the article from various wine and food producers in the area, obviously attracted by the placement beside a global brand like hers. She was surprised that her agent had agreed to it, given the forthcoming US work. She was usually more protective of the brand.

When Rachel landed, the first thing she did was phone her agent, who apparently knew nothing about the feature, and had certainly never given permission for the photos to be reproduced. The memory of her ex publishing personal photos of her around various social media came back with full force. Not that these photos were so personal, but it still felt like an invasion of her privacy. It still felt like a betrayal.

Then she rang her father. When she finished with that call, she knew exactly who'd arranged the spread. The person who'd betrayed her now had an identity. Seemed the principled Zane Black had forgotten his principles when it came to things he wanted.

~

SHE DROVE her Mini Cooper into the empty driveway. She switched off the engine and simply sat for a few minutes, trying to control the tumult of emotions which raced through her. He wasn't here. *Zane* wasn't here. Why she'd half-expected him to be, she didn't know. But relief and disappointment battled equally in her head and her heart. She opened the car door and took a deep breath. Summer had slipped away without her noticing, and there was a definite autumnal feel in the air. Leaves, now yellowed and amber, still clung to the trees, and there was a new mellowness, reminiscent of a vibrancy which had passed, of a life that had been lived, which filled the place, robbing her of her indignant mood, replacing it with a feeling of resignation.

Resignation and poignancy. Belendroit had always been about fitting in her family around her schedule. But, some time in the past six months that she'd been based there, it had become a home to her, in a way Wellington had never been. And she knew, in a big way, that that was down to Zane. But even as she acknowledged that to herself, she stopped it from becoming too important. She couldn't afford to. Once he knew what she'd done so many years before, he wouldn't want to know her.

As she got out the car, music greeted her, spilling out into the garden as per usual. A little louder now that her father was older.

She took her bag out of the boot and slammed it shut. She walked up to the veranda and saw why she hadn't been greeted. Her father lay on a sunbed, fast asleep, his mouth open. She plucked a crocheted blanket from the back of a chair and carefully lay it over him. He looked old. Much older than he did when he was awake, and she felt an overwhelming tenderness for him. How could she leave him now, even if she wanted to? He might be a mercurial man, subject to short outbursts of temper but, like a brief rainstorm, they were always followed by brilliant sunshine which only seemed brighter in contrast to the preceding gloom. He also might be vain, easily swayed by flattery, with an eye for a beautiful woman. She remembered when she was young, her mother's consternation at her father's charming ways with one woman in particular. But she doubted he would ever have acted on it. It would have broken her mother's heart and she knew her father had loved her mother dearly.

He opened his eyes suddenly and Rachel cleared her throat and blinked away the pinpricks of tears which had arisen at the memory.

"Darling!" His face lit up and her father was back. He pushed himself off the chair and gave her a hug. Then he held her at arm's length and, with his bushy eyebrows dipping in the middle, he studied her face. "What's wrong? You look like you've lost a quid and found a penny."

She smiled and pulled away. "Nothing." She looked around, unable to meet his direct gaze for fear he'd see right through her. "It's been a long week in Wellington."

"Everything sorted now? With work, I mean?"

"Yes. Amanda is pressing me to sign the US contract, but I've delayed it a month."

"A month? Oh. I hoped that… I don't know… I hoped that you might stay."

"It's an incredible opportunity, Dad."

"Yes, I'm sure," he said sadly.

"But the location for the filming hasn't been nailed down yet."

"Amanda seemed pretty keen on the idea of filming here, if I remember right."

She grinned. "And you always remember right where a pretty face is concerned, don't you, Dad?"

"It's been a lifelong hobby of mine. I don't intend to stop now."

She shook her head. "You're incorrigible." She got out her phone and scrolled through the messages. "Anything happen while I was away?"

"Happen? We're in Akaroa, don't forget, Rachel. Not a lot happens here, thank goodness."

She rolled her eyes and found Zane's number, considered calling him and then clicked off her phone. "Of course. Silly me."

"I'll go and put the kettle on." He paused on the threshold to the hall. "Unless you'd like anything stronger?"

"No, thanks. Tea will be fine."

She was slipping her phone back in her bag when her father called out from the hall. "Oh, by the way, there's a letter here for you." He emerged, brandishing it like a sword. "Don't often receive letters these days. Might be important."

Rachel took it from him. "Or it might be the opposite—junk mail."

"Or maybe *fan* mail?" he said, as he stomped toward the kitchen.

"Looks pretty official for fan mail."

She turned the letter over in her hands and glanced at the official words on the front and her heart froze. It was from the Maori tribal trust board, the people she'd approached requesting information about her child, whose name she hadn't even known at that point.

She sat in the nearest chair, heart thumping. She took a deep breath and unpeeled the gummed flap and withdrew two sheets of thick white paper.

A quick scan of the covering letter revealed that it was, indeed, about her request for information about her child. It was short and to the point—it denied her any information, or access, whatsoever.

She leaned back against the wall, as all the energy drained from her. She might know the name of her child now, but tears of frustration and rage and sadness threatened to overwhelm her, because this negative response would surely make it harder to connect with Etta. Harder, but not impossible.

She read through the second document, which was a straightforward form with the only identifying factor being her reference number, hoping against hope that she'd read it wrong. When was it dated? She looked at it again and this time she looked down at the date and signature. It was signed with the unmistakable large, legible and contained signature of Zane Black.

9

*D*espite a raging desire to drive straight over to Zane's house and vent her anger, frustration, bitter disappointment, and, simply, confusion, Rachel had retired to bed pleading a headache until her father had gone to bed. After being able to lie awake no longer with the emotions churning through her, overpowering her with first one thought, and then another, she rose, slipped on her gown and opened her door which led directly to their small, private beach.

The action of walking, the warm wind against her bare skin, lifting her silk gown, soothed her a little. Barefoot, she sank into the springy, coarse grass which became sparse as it disappeared into sand. She walked up the wooden steps of the jetty and sat on the seat at the end, looking out across the dull pewter of the smooth harbor, beyond which the hills were silhouetted against a starry sky. She'd been there a million times and yet the view had never felt more poignant. Its peace and beauty filled her and she closed her eyes and opened her mouth as if to scream. She wanted to let out the distress which churned inside her, let it dissipate into the stillness. Instead she closed her mouth.

What the hell should she do? What the hell *could* she do? Her first impulse had been to see him directly and to vent her feelings of betrayal at his signature, refusing her contact with her child, and to contest his decision. But, for once, she didn't give in to her first instinct—hadn't that always led to trouble? And it wasn't trouble she wanted, it was to see her daughter.

But she couldn't. And, maybe, just maybe, Zane was correct. Maybe it *wouldn't* be in Etta's best interests.

Rachel slipped off her robe and walked along the rough planks to the edge of the jetty where the high tide rippled around the piles, curled her toes around the edge and dived, naked, into the water. The cool water flowed along her heated skin, and she surfaced to see a crescent moon rise high above the hills. The important thing was Etta. It would be all right, she said to herself, as she flipped onto her back and kicked leisurely to shore. It *had* to be. *Etta*. It was only about Etta…

RACHEL SAT at her usual table in the window of Amber's café watching the world go by. Except she wasn't. She was looking out, unseeing, onto the early autumn afternoon. The scene was the same, no doubt *had* been the same for years, decades, generations even. But today she was looking at it with very different eyes.

"Hey, you," said Amber, sliding a coffee in front of Rachel. "What's up? You're not looking your usual chipper self." She grinned at Rachel.

Rachel tried to smile but her face didn't respond. Instead

she shook her head and brought the sugar bowl toward her and spooned a heaped spoonful into her coffee.

Amber's eyes grew larger and her smile faded. "Wow! I haven't seen you take sugar in years." She glanced around, checking out the emptying café. "Want some company?"

"Sure." Rachel couldn't summon up any more enthusiasm. She was sure her lovely sister wouldn't be able to help her—not with her unrelentingly positive attitude, nor from personal experience. No, she was on her own here.

"Cool. I'll grab a coffee."

There was a depth of ache in Rachel's heart that she'd never felt before. More so than when her ex in Wellington had betrayed her, because she now realized that this ache had been planted many years ago and had been the root cause of so much heartache afterwards. And then there was Zane. She took another spoonful and stirred it into her coffee.

Amber returned and sat down opposite on a comfy couch. She shot Rachel another look but Rachel simply shook her head and looked outside again at the trees whose leaves were fading, but not without the finale of a bright flourish of foliage.

"What are you thinking about?"

Rachel loved her sister, but sometimes her probing and sunny nature felt out of place. She looked at her—her red hair tied back in a ponytail, a trail of freckles on her delicate nose. She had the look of a Rossetti model and the nature of Pollyanna, but somehow beneath it all she was her own woman—strong and confident. Despite her air of vulnerability, Rachel suspected Amber was tougher than she was.

"Rach?" prompted Amber.

Rachel sighed. "I was looking at the trees and thinking the leaves are about to die."

"Oh, so happy thoughts then," said Amber, sipping her coffee.

Rachel didn't reply but looked out the window again, at the sun that had shifted around and now spun its bright light into her eyes, making them water.

Amber reached over and took Rachel's hand. "I'm here for you, Rachel. Whatever it is, tell me. It'll make it easier."

Rachel looked back at Amber. "Thank you, but…"

"No buts," said Amber, renewing her grip on Rachel's hand. "Look, I know I'm the baby of the family. Goodness, I mean, I was only ten when you left Akaroa for Wellington. We hardly knew each other and we haven't seen much of each other since then. But you're still my big sister, who I've always looked up to."

"Really?"

"*Yes*, really. *And* who I adore."

It was Amber's turn for her eyes to go misty and Rachel was suddenly aware of what her past had cost her, what living in Wellington had meant she'd sacrificed on the home front. She'd missed out on a close relationship with this wonderful woman.

Rachel leaned toward Amber. "And I adore you. I mean, who wouldn't? But *I* adore you most. You're my kid sister. We share a family."

"So let me help you."

Rachel bit her lip as she considered telling Amber everything. But she couldn't. There was too much at stake, not least her daughter's future. "I'll tell you what I can. How about I tell you a story?"

Amber brightened. "I love stories. Once upon a time?"

Rachel nodded. "Once upon a time there was an innocent, naive, silly girl—"

Amber frowned. "This isn't about me, is it?"

Rachel laughed. "No! It's a story, remember? Anyway, this silly girl… did something which she refused to undo and upset people close to her, people she wished she hadn't upset."

"So what did the girl do?"

"She went away."

"And... did everyone get over it?"

"Mostly everyone." She looked back at Amber. "Everyone, I suspect, except her, that is." She tilted her head to one side. "You see it so happened that the person who was upset the most, and most affected, was herself, and it took her years and lots of heartache to discover it."

"So, can she put that one thing right now? Or is it too late?"

Rachel grimaced. "I think it might be too late. Thing is, if she tried to turn back the clock and make things easier for herself, she runs the risk of making things a whole lot more difficult for someone—some *people*—she cares deeply about."

Amber exhaled and sat back in her chair. "Oh boy, that's tricky. Is there really no way round it?"

Rachel shook her head, short sharp shakes as the truth hit her. "No," she said in a whisper. She cleared her throat. "I don't think there is. I think the only way is forward. Simply to move on. Keep on doing what I was doing."

Amber smiled gently. "Keep on doing what the *girl* was doing, you mean."

Rachel frowned, momentarily confused.

"The story, remember," prompted Amber.

"Right. The girl. She has to move on and take the heartache with her. Learn to live with it."

"But maybe just knowing and accepting what happened, simply the process of trying to make things right, has helped her."

Rachel sat back, thoughtful, thinking through Amber's words. "Maybe. I guess before, it was glossed over, patched up, tried to be forgotten. But now the story has been remembered, maybe it's easier to move on." She looked at Amber, impressed. "You're right. I guess that is one way of looking at it."

The doorbell jangled as a customer entered. "You see? There's always something positive you can get from a story. Even if the story is a sad one." Amber glanced over her shoulder. "Looks like you've got company, and I've work to do."

Amber jumped up and Rachel followed Amber's gaze to Zane, who looked over with a guarded smile. She looked away quickly.

She listened as Amber chatted brightly to Zane but received only perfunctory replies. Seemed her quick look away had been noticed by Zane and while he didn't speak much to Amber, he didn't move toward her either.

"Water, please, Amber." But still he didn't come over, although she could feel his gaze on her back as if it were a laser-guided missile. Except there was no explosion, only a probing, only an enquiry as to why she wouldn't turn around and greet him, only a question as to why she was acting that way.

Then she heard Amber's tone lower as she slid a cup of coffee, in addition to the water, across the counter to Zane.

"On the house," she heard Amber say. It was followed by footsteps and Rachel closed her eyes as she felt Zane's presence looming over her. The brightness of the sun still penetrated her closed lids, she couldn't escape it, and she couldn't escape him. She looked around at the man who'd decided she couldn't see her child.

"Zane." The one syllable was cool on her lips and she could see the shock of the delivery hit Zane before he recovered and frowned.

He cocked his head to one side. "Rachel?" he responded. "You wanted to see me… your text."

"Yes."

"I was surprised, given your obvious change of heart." He shrugged. "Or mind. Is everything okay?"

She met his direct gaze. "No, it's not."

"Ah, I wondered… when you went so cool on me last week. I thought you must have had second thoughts."

"Second thoughts?" She shook her head. "It wasn't that. It wasn't about us. I'm sorry, Zane, but it's complicated."

"Want to talk about it?"

She shook her head. "No, but I have to."

"Mind if I sit down?" He indicated the empty chair opposite.

"Please do. We need to talk."

He sat down and placed his hands together on the table, ignoring his coffee. "This sounds serious. What's happened?"

"What, besides the fact that you used photos of me without my permission? Besides that?"

He frowned. "Your photos? I went to ask you but you weren't there. Jim said it would be fine."

"And is it usual to ask someone's father for permission? How old do you think I am? Sixteen?"

"No. But he said you were used to that kind of thing and suggested I simply email you."

"But you didn't."

"I asked the Tourist Board to cover it off. I'm sorry. They must have overlooked it."

She grunted and stirred her coffee. "I guess they must have."

"Is it such a big deal?"

"To me, it is. After what happened…"

"Ah," he said. "Of course. I'm sorry. It must have been a shock—reminiscent of what happened last year. I didn't think."

"No, you didn't. Still, what's one more betrayal in the scheme of things?"

Zane ducked his head so it was in line with hers, forcing her to meet his gaze. "What are you talking about? What the hell's happened?"

She met his gaze at last. "I found out something yesterday which has changed my life."

"*That* doesn't happen every day." He was trying to lighten the conversation. But some conversations couldn't be lightened. "So..." He looked around, unsure. "What exactly does that mean?"

She regarded him levelly. She should have seen it before —that uncompromising strength in every angle of his face. There was no softness where secrets could glide by, no space in his head or his heart for something imperfect, for mistakes, for mis-steps. There was only one course of action for something that was wrong and that was elimination. Now her focus had changed. Before, she'd been angry and hurt by his actions. But now she wanted him to understand exactly what he'd done.

"Zane. You know, or probably guessed, I came to Akaroa for a reason."

"Yes, you said. To move on from a series of bad relationships."

"I came here because I realized I couldn't move on, not without addressing what I should have addressed ten years ago."

"What?" He scrunched up his face in bafflement. "What are you talking about?"

She leaned forward so he could see the hurt and anger in her eyes more clearly. "I had a baby, Zane. I was sixteen years old when I had my child." She paused but there was no dawning of understanding, only shock. He tried to take her hands but she shook them off. "I had a child. It was a girl. A beautiful girl who I was pressured to give away. And I did. And I didn't look back until now, when I could no longer bear the heartache which was at the root of everything I did. I came back to find her."

There was a change in his expression. "And did you? Find her, I mean."

"Yes, I did." She paused again. "But you won't let me see her. Your brother was the father. Tommy. He and I had a child and you won't let me see her. You won't let me have a relationship with her; you won't allow me to attempt to make reparation for the mess I made when I was sixteen."

His gaze hardened and didn't leave hers. It ground into her like glass—sharp and destroying. "It was *your* application I denied."

"Yes."

"And yet you hid this fact from me all the time you've known me."

"Yes."

"And you've taken every opportunity to be with me at the school, at the marae. You were looking for her, there, weren't you?"

"Yes."

"Was that all you wanted from me?"

She paused. Was it? She opened her mouth to speak but now was the time for the truth and she didn't know what that was, anymore.

"Well, I guess that doesn't matter now, does it?" He leaned back in his chair as if he wanted to be as far away from her as possible. And she'd have believed it if it hadn't been for his eyes, which were fiercer, more demanding, more intense than ever. "You can't have what you want and so no doubt, that is why you're talking with the US producers—you're leaving, which is exactly why I denied your case. You see, Rachel, people like you have a habit of wanting to turn back the clock, jumping into someone else's life and destroying it in the process–"

"But I have no intention of destroying anything!"

He leaned forward. "And how can I know that? How can anyone know that? We can only make decisions based on the likelihood of that happening—"

"Without any personal knowledge of the people involved. How the hell does that work?"

"*Well*. It works *well*, Rachel. It happened to me and I'm not going to let it happen to Etta. You're *not* going to destroy the only family she knows, her foundation, her sense of self, her life. She's fine as she is."

She hadn't imagined he'd do that. That he'd confirm her identity. He was obviously so incensed by the whole situation that he'd let it slip.

Etta. The girl up the rugby post. The stroppy, skinny girl who Zane obviously so dearly loved and was equally infuriated by. *That* girl was her daughter. She sucked in a long breath. "So it *is* Etta."

He swore under his breath when he realized what he'd done. He ground his teeth and nodded. Once. He rubbed his index finger against his lips as he glowered at her. "I shouldn't have told you."

"You didn't. Not in so many words, anyway." She held up her hand to stop him talking. She knew what he was going to say. "You don't have to worry. I may have made more mistakes in my life than I should have done, but I *do* have a sense of right and wrong. I'm not going to contact her without permission. But I *am* going to pursue that through legal means."

"That's your prerogative. But it'll come down to the wishes of the family and we have firm principles around that."

"I don't doubt it."

"We have to do what's best for Etta."

"And you're so sure you know what that is?"

"Yes."

"How wonderful it must feel to be so sure of everything."

"I'm *not* sure of everything, but I am sure of this... of what's best for Etta."

She pressed her lips together to stop them trembling as their gaze held, full of recrimination and pain. "Etta," she said quietly. "I'd imagined many names, but not that."

He paused and then obviously made a decision. "It's short for Henrietta. I believe that was Gran's choice, rather than Tommy's."

"Yes, Tommy's role was brief, but pivotal, in the whole thing."

For all his professed certainty, Zane suddenly looked unsure. He opened his mouth to speak before closing it again. He glanced away and then back at her again. "He... didn't take advantage of you, did he?"

She shook her head with a sad smile. "I was young and curious. I rather think it was the other way around. How is he, by the way?"

"He's fine. He's living in the States with his wife and kids. Etta has visited them, but she'd rather stay here and we want her to stay, too."

"Right. So he gets the option to have her stay with him, but his own mother doesn't."

"You forfeited that right, Rachel. You gave it away. You and your parents."

"And I've lived to regret it. Every year, it gets harder."

"I'm... sorry for that. But I have to think of what's best for Etta." He pushed his fingers through his hair and glanced out the window before looking back at her. The anger had gone, replaced by distress and confusion. Rachel was surprised. She'd never seen Zane confused about anything before. Not that it mattered now.

"Etta," she repeated. "You know, I'd called her Julia. Only

to myself, of course. No one else knew. But don't worry. I'm not going to do anything. You're right. It was selfish of me to return." She rose. "But you know? I wasn't going to take her away. I didn't even want her to know who I was if it wasn't right. I simply wanted to make sure she was okay, that she wasn't wondering about me. Just to see her, to get to know her a little if I could. That's all. And that's what you've taken from me."

He ground his teeth and rose to confront her. "My family, my people, are important to me. I have a duty to protect them."

"From people who might love them?"

"From people whose love might destroy them."

"I'm not going to destroy anyone."

"Maybe not. But I can't risk it. Rules are rules, and it's my responsibility and duty to apply them."

"Rules are there to interpret, not to hide behind." She picked up her bag. "Nothing's that simple, Zane, nothing's that black or white."

Rachel didn't look back. She pulled away from Amber as she tried to reach for her and walked quickly out the door and across the road to the grass domain which lay between the café and the harbor. She'd said what she had to say and now all she could do was get away. As fast as possible.

ZANE WATCHED HER LEAVE, unable to move. He felt as if he'd been felled by a pack of rugby forwards. Adrenaline had kicked in and had masked the pain, but he sensed it in the background, and knew it would emerge when the shock had faded.

He watched her step off the pavement and narrowly miss being hit by a car which alerted her with a beep of the horn at the last moment. He started, as if to run out and rescue her. But it was too late for that. She was already moving on, crossing the road to her car, fumbling in her bag to retrieve the car keys, dropping the keys before picking them up and clicking the car open and getting inside. He continued to watch as she held her head in her hands briefly, before starting the car, and looking around, pulling out and driving off down the road.

What a mess! For a while he'd really believed that Rachel was the one for him, someone he could love and live the rest of his life with. Someone who shared his values. What a joke that was!

He rose, walked across the empty café, and reached into his wallet to pay Amber, who stood patiently watching him.

"I'm sorry, Zane. I don't know what's going on but I do know that Rachel is really devastated. She's not her usual self."

Zane shook his head, unable to answer her.

"Give her time."

He focused on entering his PIN in the machine. "Sure. She can take as much time as she likes."

Amber looked pained and bit her lip. "Surely you're not... splitting up with her?"

"I think she did that all on her own." He began to walk away and then stopped and looked back at Amber. "It doesn't mean I don't care, though. Whether I should or not, I *do* care. And if I can't be there for her, can you make sure she's okay? Please, Amber? You and Gabe? Be with her and make sure she's okay?"

"Of course. We Connellys are always there for each other. Don't worry about that. But—"

"No." He blinked and turned away. "I have to go."

He walked off without taking his receipt and was outside before she could remonstrate. He hesitated and then turned and walked toward the school. It was school holidays but some kids were playing in the playing fields, kicking balls around. He stopped and watched. Etta wasn't there but some of her mates were. He caught glimpses of their bright faces caught by the sun, laughing at something they'd done, whooping with delight when they caught the ball and ran past their opponent. They were full of life and happiness and trust in their world and that's what he wanted to keep for them. They'd have time enough when they were older to learn of life's hardships. It was up to him to make sure that that time came later rather than sooner. How could that be wrong?

But then he glanced in the direction of Belendroit, where Rachel would be arriving about now. She'd be going home, no doubt to pack, send emails, make arrangements. But she was hurting. He knew that much about her and he not only *knew* it, but *felt* it. He'd made a mistake—not in his decision about Etta, but in chasing Rachel. He'd trusted her and let down his defenses and had fallen for her. Hard. And it had shattered his black and white world, as she called it, fractured it like sunlight in rain, splitting it into so many different colors that he felt disoriented, unbalanced, for the first time in his life.

Was falling for Rachel the mistake, or had he been too blinkered by his past to misjudge his work? Was she right?

Whether Rachel was correct or not, one thing was plain: he'd protected one loved one only by hurting another.

"RACHEL?" asked Jim Connelly, who sat impatiently tapping his glasses on the side of the chair. "Are you going to tell me what happened today or am I going to have to guess?"

She glanced at him. She hardly knew what he was saying, she'd been so lost in thought, piecing together her memories of Etta, where she'd seen her in the schoolyard, the glimpse in town, putting together a puzzle to form an image which would have to see her through a lifetime.

"Sorry?"

He jumped up. "For goodness sake, Rachel. If you're not going to answer me then I might as well go out. You're behaving like a lovelorn teenager."

She smiled sadly. "Maybe I'm making up for lost time."

"What's that meant to mean?"

"You know, Dad, I know you and Mum did what you thought best at the time. But it *wasn't* the best. Not for me. And I've only come to realize that over the past year. I never had time to grieve so maybe that's what I had to do. Maybe that's what I'm doing."

She'd never seen her father look so unsure, so sad, so upset. The different expressions swept across his face like the wind ruffling the surface of the harbor. Then it settled into a glassy stillness which reflected all the sadness she felt. "I'm sorry, Rachel. I'm *so* sorry. Your mum and I, well, we didn't know what to do. You didn't want to marry the boy, or even be *with* him, and you were too young to bring up a child. You were so clever, so beautiful, you had your whole life ahead of you and we didn't want it ruined by a child."

"*My* child. *My* baby girl. How could she have ruined it, Dad?"

"It's easy for you to say that, now, looking back. But you wouldn't have had the career you've had. You wouldn't have had the chances, or the lifestyle, you can have now."

"And you know? That means so very little because I've never gotten over her."

"Rachel!"

But Rachel couldn't forgive her dad. Maybe later, but not now. Now, she had to leave and simply walk. She wanted to feel the rhythm of her body moving, walking, taking her anywhere but in that house, that bedroom, where she'd lain, watching her belly grow, imagining her future, until she'd been taken to Wellington to live with her aunt where she had her baby. Rachel's parents had taken her baby to the marae, had argued fiercely with Zane's gran who, like Zane, had said it's all or nothing. Her parents had given all and she'd ended up with nothing. And she wasn't sure she'd ever forgive them.

She continued walking up the hill behind the house, over the pastures and farmland, wanting to be higher, as high as she could, to grab some cooler air on that warm, still night. She needed to breathe.

Suddenly she could. It began to rain and she looked around, down at the harbor below her, its starlit reflection pock-marked and distorted by the rain. Then she heard the sound of people and she looked around. Her feet had taken her to the edge of the marae. She could hear the kids playing and the sound of music, she could see a community living and breathing there, but she couldn't be a part of it. She snatched a breath and thought of Zane.

She walked up to his house. No one was around but she could see a light was on. The rain was coming heavier now. She knocked on his door.

"Rachel!" He opened the door wide. "I didn't expect you."

She gave a parody of a laugh. "I hardly expected me to do this either."

"Come in, out of the rain."

She shook her head. "No. I won't be long. I wanted you to know something. In the café, earlier, you said that I must have planned this, used you to get to Etta. And I wanted you to know."

"Know what?"

The rain dripped off her hair, spattering the dry floorboards and rug darkly. "That maybe at first I was interested in you because of where you could lead me."

His mouth tightened.

"But only at first. Not later." She stepped away from him before her faulty instincts took over and she pressed her wet cheek to his chest and held herself there until he put his arms around her. She took another step away. "Goodbye, Zane." She ran down the steps, splashing across the puddles, before disappearing into the bush which would take her back to Belendroit.

ZANE STOOD under the outside light, against which the moths darted and batted themselves, watching Rachel stumble across the muddy ground toward the path which led back down to the shore and Belendroit. He fought with all his strength not to run after her and help her—to stop her stumbling, to stop her hurting, but most of all to stop her from leaving him. And his strength won.

He walked back inside, automatically tracking toward the kitchen, where he gripped the bench and looked down, imagining Rachel half-running, half-stumbling back down the path toward the coast road and then on to Belendroit. Then he looked up and out the window which looked down on the marae. Lights were on in the houses which clustered around it, and on inside the marae itself where people gathered to talk and eat. *This* was what it was all about, he reminded himself. Keeping his people safe. He shook his head and turned his back to the lights. Instead, he looked out the far windows toward the dark trees. Rain spattered fitfully against the glass. But who was keeping Rachel safe? And why wasn't it him?

10

*Z*ane passed his grandmother a cup of tea. She waved her hand for him to place it on the table beside her, not looking away from the TV screen.

"Gran! Can you leave that? I assume you asked me over for more than to make you a cup of tea." He gestured to a couple of his nieces who were painting their nails outside on the deck in the autumn sunshine. "Something which one of the girls could have done."

Gran glanced up at him. "Do I need an excuse to see my favorite grandson?"

"We're all your favorites, or so you say." He tried, unsuccessfully, to hide a grin in response to her persuasive smile. She grabbed his hand and kissed it and, holding it tight, turned back to the TV. He perched on the side of her chair, unable either to refuse his charming gran, or to pull his hand away from her strong grip. "What's so engrossing anyway?"

"It's a documentary."

He watched as teenage girls sat in a classroom. The only thing strange about this as far as he could see was that their age varied and they were focusing intently. Then the class finished and, instead of going out into the yard to gossip, the girls went to a creche where they picked up their children, nursed them and played with them. "What kind of school is this?"

"It's a school for single mothers. In Wellington. The kids go to school with their mums and are looked after in the same place while their mums can study. Cool, eh?"

"Yeah, but I haven't heard of it."

"Not many of the schools around. Funding is difficult for them."

Then Zane peered forward as he listened to a voiceover describing how, apart from a small amount of government funding, the schools relied on patrons. Slowly the camera panned over the girls and focused on the person at the front of the room, doing some kind of demonstration. "What the hell?"

He received a slap on his thigh. "Don't swear."

He ignored her and reached for the remote control and increased the volume, and what he saw, and heard, had him frozen to the spot. It was Rachel, doing what looked like a cookery demonstration to the teenagers who were hanging on her every word, laughing, interacting and having a ball. Then the scene ended and Rachel was interviewed. Her passion for supporting these girls who otherwise would have to give up either their education, or their child, shone through. She ended the interview saying that no one should have to make such a choice. Then she gave a quick, uncertain glance to camera and Zane's heart clenched as he saw the depth of pain and strength in those big brown eyes: Rachel's eyes, Etta's eyes.

"I didn't know."

"Of her involvement? Maybe she didn't tell many people. Sure looks like what she's doing is making a difference to these people—morale and money."

He opened his mouth to speak, but shook his head instead. He didn't know what to think anymore. He looked down into his grandmother's eyes which looked up to him.

"I misjudged her, Zane. I'm a proud woman and, after what happened, I didn't want anything to do with the Connelly family. But maybe I was wrong."

"You were right, Gran. *Then*, anyway. Etta needed a secure upbringing and you gave her that. But now? I don't know either anymore."

"Don't you, boy? Then you should. She's proved herself twice over—once by coming home and making contact through the board, and twice by this." She pointed to the TV. "Rachel's been trying to make up for her and her parents' decision ever since. And she has, for those girls, at least. But not for herself. Maybe it's time to help her make peace with herself?"

He shook his head, as much as in confusion as denial. "She's leaving."

"Leaving? Then make her change her mind. Her place is here."

"And how do you propose I do that?" He paced the floor. "On behalf of the board I've refused her access to Etta. We're not talking now."

The old lady watched him for a few moments before reaching around her neck and taking off the greenstone pendant she always wore. "Zane, my beautiful *mokopuna*." She pushed herself off the settee and rose to her full height which barely reached five feet. Zane could never understand how such a short woman could be so commanding. "You need to do something you've never done before—except on the sports field—and let your instinct guide you. Life's been tough for you, but it's about time you loosened up a bit. Start with Rachel. I believe she's a good woman." She held out the pendant. "Take this *taonga*."

"I can't take that! It's yours, it's always been in the female line of the family."

"And it will continue to be. I want you to take it and give it to the woman you love. It's yours to treasure. Just like she is."

He held his grandmother's steady gaze as he accepted the *taonga* from her, as everything fell into place. "Thank you."

ZANE STOOD, hands on hips, facing his niece who rammed the last piece of toast into her mouth before picking up a ball and hurling it against the wall of her great grandmother's wooden house and catching it expertly. "Why do I have to go?" asked Etta.

"Because I said so," said Zane sternly.

"But I don't get it." Etta scowled and threw the ball again, caught it and threw it again with a repetitive thud which was getting on Zane's nerves.

"You don't have to *get* it. All you have to do is come with me."

Again the dull thud of the ball. "Who else is going?"

Zane thought quickly. She'd suspect if it were only her. "A couple of others, and you and me."

She shot him a quick look before throwing the ball over-arm this time, her lips pursing with angry concentration. "Just us, and this woman you want me—I mean *us*—to meet."

Zane glanced around, and then back to his niece. Nothing got past her. "Yes."

She bounced the ball on the ground, held on to it tight and looked at him directly for the first time, with Rachel's eyes. Why hadn't he seen it before? "Why?"

He sighed. Trust Etta. Direct and to the point. There was no way he was going to get Etta there without telling her something that made sense to her. She was too smart—street-smart in a way he suspected was more to do with his half-brother than Rachel—and intelligent which was *all* to do with Rachel. "Because… I think you'll all enjoy meeting her. She's a chef."

"I hate cooking." She threw the ball against the wall again.

"Then all the more reason to meet her and learn something."

"So I'm going because I need to learn how to cook? Because *we* need to cook," she added sarcastically. "I thought you went to kitchens to do that. But we're going to a café to eat."

"She's my friend, Etta. And I want you to meet her."

"Because you're dating?" She smiled for the first time. "That's what the others said."

"Whatever they said, they're wrong."

"How can you know they're wrong when you don't know what they said?"

He stepped away. He'd had enough of dealing with someone who, he suspected was capable of running verbal rings around him. "I'll pick you up, and the others, after school on Friday."

"Sure. It'll be good to meet your *girlfriend*, Uncle Zane."

Zane was about to deny it, then thought better of it, especially when she gave that wide grin which lit up her face, transforming the dark glower to a bright cheekiness which charmed everyone she deigned to reveal it to. He shook his head and walked to his car.

The day was misty and the sun was trying to penetrate the cloud, creating soft rainbow arcs in the sky. He'd hardly slept that night, going over and over the assumptions and beliefs that he'd held so close, lived his life by, all these years. They'd kept him safe and sane and he'd assumed they'd do the same for his family and whanau—his people. But, if that was the case, why was his heart breaking at what his decision had done to Rachel? The pain had been visible in her face that night when she'd arrived in the rain—a pain that ground deep inside, from which he knew he'd never recover.

He'd been intensely attracted to Rachel from the first moment he'd seen her. He'd *liked* her from their first conversation. And he'd seen a future with her from their first date. But he hadn't stopped to examine his feelings, hadn't thought about untrustworthy words like "love". He'd heard enough about love when he'd been a high-profile rugby player. Everyone, including his girlfriend, had told him they'd loved him. But it had come to nothing, and had taught him not to trust words.

But Rachel's pain had forced him to look deep inside, at his feelings, and at his rigid views. And he'd emerged a different man. He still might not trust words, but he'd show Rachel that she could trust his actions. Starting that morning. He looked once more at the gray light which had been split into every color under the sun, and knew it was the right decision.

THE REMAINS of the mist were evaporating into thready trails above the harbor as Rachel returned from her early morning walk. She'd spent the last few days organizing a series of meetings the following week in the States. Her agent said the only unknowns were how many series they wanted, rather than whether they wanted them at all. Rachel couldn't help thinking it would be nice to go somewhere where she was wanted for a change.

She walked up the steps to the veranda—empty at that hour, her father was getting up later now, as he grew older— and her phone beeped. She pulled it out of her back pocket and squinted at the screen as the sun broke through the cloud and obscured it. She retreated into a corner, under the overhanging leaves of the wisteria which was wet with dew, and stared at the screen. An email message from Zane.

She opened it and quickly scanned it. Then she sat, oblivious to the dewy seat, and re-read the message, the full force of its meaning slowly forming. He'd invited her to tea at the café. Amber's café. But not by himself. He was bringing three kids with him. A treat for them, he'd explained, to mark the end of term. He'd included their names but there had been only one name which struck her. Etta. What the hell?

She double-checked her other messages and texts to see if there was some kind of earlier message which would explain things. But there was nothing.

She wandered inside as if in a dream, her mind darting from one idea to the other, discarding them as quickly as they came. But all her thoughts kept returning to the first thought she had. It could only mean one thing—a chance. Maybe Zane was giving her a chance to connect with her child.

But still, there was little warmth in the email, a simple invitation to meet at the café, no apologies, no words of understanding or regret. Only an invitation to meet in a few days' time. Friday. A day of the year which held special significance to her.

She squashed the small glimmer of hope before it had a chance to burn brightly. Gabe may have told Zane that she'd booked her flights—first to Wellington and then on to the States—and she was leaving Akaroa after the weekend. Most likely this was a small olive branch, a way to say goodbye. Safety in numbers. A glimpse at what might have been.

She couldn't allow herself to read anything more into it, she reminded herself as she read through the cool words. Nothing.

She typed a reply, deleted it and retyped it several times, before deciding on a brief, impersonal acceptance.

Her phone went and she answered it as she walked through the house to her bedroom which was piled with boxes. She sat amongst them as she listened to her agent talk her through her exciting new future—a future which held little allure for Rachel, only a kind of bleak inevitability.

FRIDAY AFTERNOON SEEMED to take forever to arrive. Rachel had been dreading, and eagerly anticipating it, in equal measure. She'd filled her week catching up with her family and working on her proposals for her new shows. And, while she worked on her laptop in the kitchen/family room, she'd look up from time to time at the kitchen which still contained some of the remnants of the earlier filming. And she remembered how happy she'd been and how right her new ideas had felt about filming at Belendroit. The new US proposals were similar, but would be filmed in a studio, made to look like Belendroit's kitchen—*that*, her agent had insisted on. Rachel had never felt so far away from reality as now—recreating her reality in a false environment. She couldn't help thinking of Zane wanting a real life, and finding it here, in Akaroa. The option she'd chosen emphasized how false her world was. The contrast couldn't have been more poignant, or pointed.

And now it was Friday and all she could think about was what to wear.

Her father looked at her over his reading glasses. "That's the third change of outfits in half an hour. What's going on, Rachel? Finding it hard to decide what to wear to see your sister?"

She threw him an irritated look. "It's this change in weather. One minute it's hot, the next cool."

"It's called autumn."

"It's called annoying."

He shook his head. "Whatever the weather, that outfit"—he stabbed his finger at Rachel's conservative dark gray dress which fitted like a glove but had all the allure of a nun's habit—"will be like a dark cloud has moved in and obscured the sun. What about that pretty frock you wore ten minutes ago."

"It's too young."

"You *are* young."

"Not *that* young."

"In that outfit you look like some school child's version of what an old-fashioned mother looks like. Even your grandmother didn't look like that!" He rose stiffly from his chair and dropped the newspaper on the table. He walked over to Rachel and cupped her face. "Whatever it is you're up to, be yourself, for goodness sake. Because you are a wonderful girl and you need to show people the real you."

She huffed. "The real me! Is there any such thing?"

"Somewhere beneath that drab dress, yes, there is." He kissed her on the cheek. "Now, you go and get ready to see... Amber, was it?" He grinned but didn't wait for an answer. "While I get ready for my rehearsal at the theatre."

As Rachel changed once more, she pondered on her father's words. He was right. Of course he was right. And for once he didn't push things. He knew something was up but, for whatever reason, he wasn't going to get involved. She looked at herself in the mirror. Well, only insofar as he wanted to make sure she didn't look dowdy; he wanted her to look herself. She looked up into her eyes and smiled. And, of course, he was right. If there was ever a time to reveal her true self, it was now.

RACHEL REGRETTED ARRIVING EARLY. It increased the nerves she'd been battling all week. The café was busy and every time she caught someone's eye she felt heat flare in her cheeks, as if she'd been caught out. Over the years she'd become accustomed to her fame, and was generally able to ignore it unless people accosted her directly. But here, now, she felt like she'd been caught out doing something she shouldn't have been doing. Or maybe, something she didn't deserve. Or, even more likely, it was because she sat alone, under festoons of ribbons, draping from a central point clustered with balloons above the table, so it was like she was contained in a teepee made of ribbons.

And then there was the table—beautifully laid by Amber —complete with an old-fashioned tiered cake platter, crammed with the yummiest cream confections, tiny, rich chocolate cakes and rose pink-iced fairy cakes, as well as antique, gold-rimmed plates piled with delicate sandwiches. It was fit for a party—a girl's birthday party.

Rachel knew what the date was. It was a date that she'd marked—celebrated wasn't the right word—every year for the past ten years. Zane was including Rachel in Etta's birthday celebrations. But whether Etta was aware of Rachel's identity, she didn't know.

Rachel folded her arms and then unfolded them, clasping her clammy hands in her lap as she peered out the window. Then her heart stopped. Three children were running across the road ahead of Zane. He shouted at them but only two of them slowed to a walk. Etta arrived first at the door which tinkled the old-fashioned bell. She glanced at her uncle, obviously expecting a reprimand, but Zane simply shook his head and she ran up to the counter.

Instinctively Rachel rose in her seat and watched her

daughter. But Etta didn't come to her. "Amber!" shouted Etta, as she ran over to Amber and gave her a hug.

Rachel looked away, absurdly hurt. She had no idea that Amber and Etta knew each other. And not only knew each other, but obviously really liked each other. But it wasn't only about her. Rachel felt a stab of regret for Amber, too. Amber had been too young to know of Rachel's pregnancy and, as far as Rachel knew, was still unaware of it and Rachel's relationship to Etta. And there she was, being affectionate with a girl who was her niece and she had no clue.

Guilt consumed Rachel as she suddenly realized how the decision taken ten years before had affected more than herself and her child. She'd robbed Amber of a niece.

When she tore her gaze from Etta and Amber she saw that Zane was watching her carefully. He'd also dressed up for the occasion in smart trousers and a white shirt. Rachel briefly wondered if Zane ever looked anything but impressive. But she knew he didn't. *He* wore his clothes, rather than the other way around, because he was comfortable with who he was and had no need to impress. And of course, for that very reason, he did impress.

He came over to her, hesitated briefly, and kissed her on the cheek. "It's good to see you."

She forced an uncomfortable smile. "And you."

He frowned. "Are you sure?"

She bit her lip and glanced over at Etta and her two friends. "Of course." She smiled again, but suspected it was no less convincing. "And thank you." She glanced at Etta. "For the invitation."

"You're welcome."

"It… couldn't have been easy."

"No, not easy, but then doing the right thing rarely is."

She frowned. "The right thing?" She wanted him to elaborate, to ask him what he *really* meant, but she couldn't find the words.

"You don't have to do this if you don't want to, Rachel. Etta is none the wiser. It's for you, before you go."

"Of course I want to." Her words tumbled out. "There's nothing else I want. Especially today of all days."

"Okay. But she doesn't know and I don't want her to. You do understand that?"

"Yes, of course. And, thank you, I really appreciate it. After everything that's happened, I didn't think I'd get to spend any time with her. You're bending your rules, I think."

He shrugged. "I don't know about bending. Ignoring them, more like."

"Uncle Zane!" Etta shouted and they both turned to her, Zane's words and their meaning swirling unformed in Rachel's head. Before she could ask him more, the children had descended on them, bringing Amber with them.

Etta and her friends squeezed up along the bench. Etta sat opposite Zane, while Rachel sat by the window, opposite the two boys. They all listened to Amber's imaginative description of the menu. Amber had a gift for creating worlds—with her art and her words—and it was a gift which Rachel had never thought much of until now, as she watched the looks of wonder on the children's faces. Amber's blue eyes were wide, lost in the world of words she was creating. Something to do with *Alice Through the Looking Glass* and a feast to rival the Mad Hatter's Tea Party.

"Can we choose anything?" asked Etta.

"Yes, whatever you like," replied Zane. "It's your birthday, after all."

"As well as cake, there's pizza, chips, the usual," said Amber. "Zane? Hot chocolate for you?" she asked with a grin.

Etta laughed. "He hates that stuff."

"I'm being ganged up against. Just water, thanks Amber."

With virtually everything on the menu ordered, the two boys kept up a continual stream of banter, with Etta, initially shy, chipping in and glancing often and suspiciously at Rachel. Slowly she loosened up and began to join in the boys' conversation, leaving Zane and Rachel to talk politely about Rachel's forthcoming trip. But it couldn't be sustained and, after Etta relaxed, Rachel sat back and observed her while making sure to give equal attention to the boys, so as not to arouse suspicion.

It wasn't until the end of the meal, when Zane had excused himself to settle up the bill, that Etta suddenly looked up at Rachel. "Are you going out with Zane?"

"No. I mean I was. But—"

"But not now? How could you leave him? All my aunties say he's crazy in love with you."

Rachel widened her eyes in surprise. "Well… I think your aunties might have misunderstood."

"My aunties know everything, about everything."

"I'm sure they do. But, um, in this case, I'm not so sure." She groped for something to say which could change the subject. "Anyhow, I have to leave for the States on Monday."

"Why?"

"Because…" Rachel shrugged. "I have work to do."

"People work here. Why can't you?"

Rachel softened and leaned forward, toward Etta. "Would you like me to?"

"I don't care. But Zane does." With no idea that she had just stabbed Rachel in the heart, Etta jumped up, closely followed by the others and they walked out of the café, shouting their goodbyes to Amber as they went. She watched them cross the street and tried to swallow the lump in her throat. Then Etta glanced at her through the window and gave her a hesitant wave before running off into the park. Etta wouldn't have seen Rachel's answering wave, nor the tears that followed. But, when she turned back to the café, Zane did.

He sat down and put an arm around her, not caring what gossip it might ignite. "Rachel, I'm sorry. I didn't mean to upset you. I thought you'd want this."

She fumbled in her bag for a tissue and blotted away the mascara from under the eyes. "I *did* want this. It was wonderful—one of the best moments of my life."

"Well, I'm not sure that it qualifies for that!" he said, trying to joke. "It doesn't say much for the rest of your life." His face fell as she started to cry again. He stroked her hair. "Rachel! I'm sorry. I always say the wrong things. I only want to cheer you up. Not make you sad."

She sniffed and took a deep breath. "Today was wonderful but it's made me see what I haven't seen all along. It's too late to be a part of her life, isn't it?"

He hesitated and then nodded. "I think so. I don't want her hurt."

"Only me."

His eyes flickered over her face and he shook his head. "No, of course not. I don't want you hurt either."

"But that was done a long time ago, I guess. And I did it all by myself." She rose to leave. "Thank you again, Zane. I'll treasure this memory."

She walked away quickly, not wanting him to see her cry again.

ZANE SWEPT up the remaining assignments on his desk and into his bag and took a last look around the classroom before switching off the lights. He was about to exit the room when a movement outside the window caught his eye. He walked over and looked out. Etta was standing with her hands on her hips as a boy writhed on the ground in front of her holding his nose while another boy backed away. Zane flung open the window. "Etta!" The boys looked around but she didn't. "I want to see you, now!"

Still she didn't turn around but she'd heard him. He could tell by the jut of her jaw as she walked to the school room. He frowned. She'd always been fiery, but she didn't usually initiate fights.

He went to the kitchen and grabbed an icepack from the freezer and went over to the group. The boy was now standing, blood running from his nose. He told the boy what to do, and placed the bag over the bridge of his nose. "Not broken." He glared at Etta. "*You*. Inside. We need to talk."

Etta's fierce eyes still flashed angry darts at the boy, and at Zane, but she walked with her head held high into the classroom.

When Zane returned to the classroom, he found Etta beside the open door, arms folded, leaning against the wall, with a mutinous look on her face.

He closed the door gently. He knew, deep down, that whatever Etta had done, she'd done for good reason. He needed to find out what that reason was, and try to make her see that lashing out wasn't good. His brother's daughter had a hot head, exactly like him. But he was going to make damn sure that it didn't land Etta into the kind of trouble his brother had gotten himself into.

He rested against his desk and folded his arms, echoing her stance. "So what was that all about?"

She glowered at him with her beautiful dark eyes and looked down again, as if the scuffed floor was endlessly fascinating.

He dipped his head and caught her gaze as she flashed him a quick look. "Etta," he said encouragingly. "You know you're not going to leave here until you tell me what happened, so you might as well do us both a favor by telling me straight away."

He watched her lowered gaze flicker from one scuffed point on the floor to another as she thought it through. She licked her lips. He was getting through to her.

"It was them, they started it."

"How? What did they do?"

"They didn't *do* anything."

He sighed. Seemed like he was going to have to ask exactly the right question to get any kind of answer. "Okay, what did they *say*?"

She shrugged.

"If you don't tell me, I'll ask them. I'll find out one way or another, and I'd prefer to find out from you first."

She screwed her lips up as if she'd eaten something sour. "Stupid Jake. I told him he was a liar."

"Etta," he warned.

She looked up sharply, eyes flashing. "He told me that that Rachel woman was my mum, and I told him he was a liar!"

He blinked at the hurt she'd felt, feeling it right along with her. He had to tell her something that he'd wanted to shelter her from. For the first time he wondered if he'd been wrong. Seemed word had gotten out—so much for confidential board papers, so much for his grandmother's ability to keep a secret—and had made things worse… much worse.

Her eyes narrowed as she watched him. "She isn't, is she?"

He grimaced. "Yes, she is."

Her eyes narrowed further and she gritted her teeth. "Then why didn't she tell me? She should have told me. Or you. You could have told me."

"Etta." He placed his hand on her shoulder. "It's complicated."

"No, it's not. She's my mum and I didn't know. That's simple."

He groaned inwardly. Of all his extended family, Etta was by far the brightest, and the feistiest. He knew she wouldn't accept anything less than the whole unvarnished truth. She could smell a rat a mile away. "I know it seems simple to you, but it wasn't. Rachel"—the name was met with a scowl—"had you when she was very young, too young to cope and everyone thought it for the best for you to be raised by your father's family."

"Good. I don't ever want to see that woman again."

The thought of Rachel hearing these words made him wince. "You don't mean that."

"I do," Etta muttered, staring at the floor again.

"Etta! She was only five years older than you are now, when she became pregnant. Think of *your* dreams, think of what you'd have to sacrifice for a child."

"I wouldn't be stupid enough to get pregnant." She jerked her head to the boys she hung out with who were clustered in the field waiting for her to emerge. "There's no way I'd do anything like that anyhow. It's disgusting."

Zane swallowed the grin. "Your feelings on that will change."

"No, they won't," she muttered.

"Anyhow, you shouldn't be hard on her. She was only a child herself."

"So what? And now she thinks she can come back and claim me."

"Has she claimed you?"

"No."

"Then I think you're wrong, don't you?"

She looked up at him then, with eyes which held no defenses, in which he could see the raw hurt, in eyes that were exactly like Rachel's. He swallowed down a lump.

"Then why has she come back?"

"Because she wanted to find you—she didn't know your

identity—and to see you, if possible, to make sure you're okay. Etta, she wanted to make contact with you, but was scared of disrupting your life. She went through the proper channels to try to make contact with you."

Etta scrunched up her nose. "And?"

"And… she was refused."

"Who refused her? Why?"

"Me. I did."

Etta stepped back as if he'd punched her. She opened the door and paused, her fingers gripping the door frame. Then she continued through and ran outside.

"Etta!" Zane shouted as he watched her run across the grass, away from her mates and toward the sea. The boys were about to follow but he waved them away. "Let her go," he called out and the boys obeyed, uncertainly, and began kicking a ball around. He watched her walk down the street until she got to Beach Road and then she disappeared. He knew where she was going. The same place he used to go when he wanted peace, down to the sea.

He went back inside the classroom and pulled his phone from his pocket. He walked to the window and gazed out, as he raked his hands through his hair. Like it or not, he had a phone call to make.

RACHEL PUT down the phone with shaking hands. Despite what Zane had told her, there was a part of her which was immensely relieved. Her daughter knew her identity. Wasn't that what she'd wanted all along? Of course, but not under such conditions. She was angry with Zane for that. The news must have been leaked from his board of trustees. If he'd simply granted her permission, it wouldn't have happened like this.

Like a robot, Rachel filled the kettle. As it came to the

boil, she looked out across the familiar scene, imagining what Etta must be feeling, imagining what she must be thinking. From what Zane had said, Etta was in shock and angry. That was only too natural, but Rachel couldn't help imagining scenarios where they'd move past that, and where they could meet and, eventually, have a proper relationship. It was bad news for Zane, upsetting news for Etta, but for all that, it was news that inflated a huge bubble of hope inside Rachel.

She glanced at the clock. Her father wouldn't be back for a while. She'd postpone her flight to the States. She needed time to sort things out with Etta.

She'd only just finished her emails, cancelling her flights to Wellington and then on to the US when she heard running footsteps coming from the beach side of the house. Then footsteps slammed up the veranda steps and the door burst open. A tall, skinny kid stood silhouetted against the after-noon sun, hands on hips.

"Etta!" Rachel stepped toward her.

Etta stabbed her finger at her. "Don't come anywhere near me!"

Rachel froze to the spot, her stomach in knots. "Etta, I—"

"I haven't come here to listen to you. I've come here to tell you I don't want anything to do with you. I want you to go away."

"Etta… I'm not going anywhere yet. Not until we've had a chance to talk. Your uncle rang and told me you found out. I'm so sorry."

"I don't care if you're sorry. *You* didn't want me when I was born and *I* don't want *you* now."

The knot twisted tighter in Rachel's gut. "I understand." She wrung her hands, trying to think what she could say to this girl who she'd wronged so many years before.

"How can you? Your mum didn't disown you."

"It wasn't like that. It was complicated."

"That's what Uncle Zane said, and it's bullshit." Etta began to back out the door. "Bullshit," she repeated.

Rachel stepped toward her, her heart aching for this girl, *her* child, a stranger. "Etta, I'm so sorry. I never meant for this to happen like this. I never meant for you to be hurt. I'm so sorry."

Etta shook her head and ran off. Rachel followed her but caught hold of the veranda post and clung to it. "Etta," she half-whispered, as she watched the girl run back the way she'd come, across the short lawn, down to the bay and disappear along the beach toward town. She vowed then and there that she'd do whatever it took to make amends to her daughter—even if it mean never having a relationship with her. Even if it meant losing her forever.

11

*R*achel's decision to film the new series at Belendroit had been welcomed by the US studios. But whether it was welcomed by Zane or Etta, Rachel had no idea. The months had passed with only limited contact from Zane. But Rachel had no choice but to stay. She had Etta to consider now—whether Etta wanted her to, or not.

In the end it had been Zane who persuaded her to stay—to not simply delay her flight, but to cancel it indefinitely. And it hadn't been any emotional plea either on behalf of himself or Etta. It had been the plain fact that Rachel had left Etta once and, even if Etta had declared the opposite, Rachel *had* to stay for Etta's sake now. Whether Etta knew it or not, she needed to have Rachel be there for her. Leaving New Zealand wouldn't solve any problems; staying might, just might, help solve them. And so Rachel had stayed.

She'd watched the weeks turn into months as the autumn colors deepened and disappeared under the cooler skies of early winter. She received regular updates from Zane as to how Etta's counseling sessions were going. Slowly, it seemed. But she received nothing more from him—no casual visits, no requests for dates, no accidentally-on-purpose meetings. He'd cooled things between them, presumably because he was no longer interested in Rachel. She had to face the fact that she'd ultimately proved to be exactly the sort of person Zane had been trying to avoid—a person with a very public profile who'd proved untrustworthy and a threat to his family and whanau.

So when there was a knock at the door one damp evening, as the night was starting to fall, she was surprised to see his recognizable silhouette behind the glass panes of the door, illuminated by the outside light. She opened the door. "Zane!"

If he smiled, she couldn't see. His expression was shadowed by the bright light behind him.

"Rachel."

"I... didn't expect to see you."

He glanced down. "No." There was a long pause.

"Rachel!" Her father called from down the hall. "Who is it?"

She half-turned. "It's... Zane."

"Zane? Well, let him inside, then."

"Oh, right. Of course." She opened the door wide, allowing a few moths to flutter into the hall. "Sorry... I..." For once in her life she had no idea what to say, as thought after thought, hope after hope, was swiftly sabotaged by common sense.

"Thanks." He stepped into the hall and waited for her to lead them into the old-fashioned drawing room which the family still used as their main living area. Rachel walked inside where Jim sat next to a roaring fire. He rose to greet Zane.

"Good to see you, my boy. What have you been up to? Hardly seen you around!"

"I've been busy, Jim." Zane glanced at Rachel.

"Would you like a drink of something? Tea, coffee?" asked Rachel.

"We can do better than that!" Jim said to Zane. "Have a glass of wine. I've some very good Pinot Noir you should taste. And stay for dinner. It's one of the recipes which Rachel has been testing. All about comfort food apparently. She's been relentlessly feeding anybody and everybody over the past months. You'll be doing us both a favor by eating it. I'm totally comforted now and have no further need for more. Although I'm not so sure the same could be said of everyone else around here." He shot Rachel a meaningful glance.

"It's for the new show," she said defensively.

"Your new show?" Zane asked Rachel. "You're still going ahead with it, then?"

Rachel felt confused. "Yes, of course. It's my job."

"Oh. Only I thought..." He shook his head and spoke directly to Jim. "I don't want to intrude."

"Nonsense. You must stay."

Zane hesitated, his eyes fixed questioningly on Rachel.

Jim looked from one to the other. "Mustn't he, Rachel?"

She cleared her throat. "Of course."

Zane gave a brief half-smile. "In that case, yes, thank you, I'll stay."

"Good," said Jim. "Come and talk to me by the fire. After all, it's thanks to you that we have a huge pile of chopped wood. Update me on everything."

"I'll get us some drinks," said Rachel, slipping out the door, needing a respite from the chaotic emotions which seeing Zane had stirred. She couldn't think why Zane had come after all these months. Was it to warn her off altogether? Was it to tell her to leave, that things had worsened? That Etta hated her more than ever? Rachel had no idea. But she needed reinforcements. She slipped into her bedroom and rang Gabe's number.

After a brief one-sided chat with Gabe—which consisted of her telling him to come, immediately—she brought a bottle of wine and four glasses into the drawing room.

"Four glasses?" Jim asked Rachel.

"Oh, yes. Gabe's coming to dinner."

"Oh, good. So, Zane, what have you been up to since we last saw you? Family's well, I hope?"

"Yes, thank you. Gran is the same. The rest of the family are thriving." He glanced at Rachel and then back to Jim.

"And Etta?" asked Jim.

Typical, thought Rachel. If there was an elephant in the room, Jim would draw attention to it.

"She's fine, thanks." Rachel watched him carefully. She noticed the slight frown and pressing of his lips together. She doubted anyone else would. "Well, no, she's not. She's had a few issues. But the counselor reports an improvement."

"Oh!" The breath was snatched from her body. It wasn't until both Zane and Jim looked sharply at her that Rachel realized she'd spoke out loud. "How?" She swallowed dryly. "How is she improving? How is she doing?"

Zane glanced back at Jim and looked uncomfortable and didn't answer immediately. She suddenly couldn't bear it— she couldn't bear to think what Zane's silence meant, and couldn't bear to think of the pain she'd caused her child.

She jumped up. "I have to go and prepare dinner." She walked quickly over to the door, aware that both Zane and her father were silently watching her. Let them. She couldn't stay in the room where all the silence told her was how she was responsible for devastating the life of her child.

"Rachel!" said Zane. She held open the door, firmly declaring her intention, but turned to him at the last moment. What was he going to do? Recount all her faults, all the things she'd done wrong, before her father? It seemed unlikely. Talk about Etta? Even more unlikely.

"Yes?"

"Can I help you?" He rose. "In the kitchen, I mean."

"What? No. I'm fine." She took another step through the door.

"I came to tell you something. And I want to tell you now." He glanced between Jim and Rachel.

"Don't mind me," said Jim. "I'll disappear if you want me to."

"Don't go, Dad," said Rachel. She didn't want to know the dismal truth and she somehow felt that her father's presence might prevent it.

Jim looked uncomfortable but Zane looked back at Rachel with a shrug. "Okay. I came to tell you that the board has approved your revised application."

"What?" Rachel was stunned. "What revised application? I didn't revise it!"

"I"—he paused and took a deep breath—"took the liberty of making certain revisions to enable it to be passed."

"Really? And did you intend to tell me this at some point?"

"Yes. Now. I've come direct from the meeting." Zane was watching her intently. "I thought you might be pleased."

"Of course I am. But I thought I might have some input into the process."

"I'm sure," said Jim, "that Zane knows the process somewhat better than you, Rachel."

"Maybe. But Rachel's right. I should have consulted her. But I didn't want to raise your hopes. I couldn't anticipate the decision of the other board members."

"And what exactly was the final decision?"

"That, subject to the usual considerations and constraints

under the Guardianship Act, you will be able to make contact with Etta."

"And these constraints?" There had to be a catch somewhere.

"They're concerned with the family, with Etta. And the family won't oppose any approach from you. It's simply Etta, and her counsellor's report, that needs to be considered."

"Oh!" Rachel gasped, as she stepped through the door, pulling it closed behind her. She continued on to the kitchen, consumed by a strange mix of grief and relief. It wasn't until minutes later, when she felt her father's hand on her shoulder that the sobs emerged. They arose from some deep place she'd carefully concealed, from everyone, including herself. But Zane's words had blown the seal, and there was nothing but raw emotion now and, with her father's arm around her, there was no stopping it.

ZANE WONDERED whether he should follow Rachel and Jim through into the kitchen, but thought better of it. If Rachel had wanted his company, she'd have stayed. He hadn't anticipated this. He'd imagined she'd be ecstatic—overjoyed to have the last hurdles to her relationship with Etta overthrown. But this... He took a sip of wine and grimaced as the door opened. But it wasn't Rachel, it was Gabe, unaware of the scene taking place between Rachel and her father.

Gabe frowned. "So what brings you to Belendroit? I thought you'd be at that meeting—the big hui in Christchurch. It's all over the news."

"I was. And I will be. But I wanted to see Rachel."

Gabe glanced toward the sound of Rachel's voice, and Jim's remonstrances, and winced. "She's not in a good place right now. You might want to leave it."

"Because she's busy?" Zane asked hopefully.

Gabe shook his head. "Uh-uh. *You*, mate. *You*. You killed her dreams."

It was Zane's turn to wince. He shook his head. "I didn't know it was Rachel who was looking for Etta, no idea they were *her* dreams."

"And would that have made a difference?" Gabe was uncharacteristically cool but Zane couldn't hold it against him. He'd asked himself the same question repeatedly over the past few months.

"No, it wouldn't."

"So if you haven't changed your mind, why are you here? Rachel's devastated and to be frank, you're the last person she wants to see."

"I have changed my mind. And I've changed the board's mind. The decision has been overturned, that's what I've just told her."

Gabe frowned. "I don't understand. You said it wouldn't have made any difference if you'd known it was her."

"It wouldn't. But because of what I feel for her, I saw, for the first time, things from her point of view. And once I'd caught a glimpse of her heartache and her need and desire to set things right, I couldn't go back. She changed my mind for me."

"Jesus! That must have been like making a lawnmower undertake a slalom. Would have churned up the ground—not a pretty sight."

"It sure felt like it. But, seriously, Gabe, she opened my eyes and made me realize that I couldn't carry on, doing what I was doing, trying to protect my whanau from the outside world, assuming it would be bad for it." He threw his hands in the air. "I mean, how in God's world could Rachel be bad for Etta?"

"But you didn't know it was Rachel."

"No. And I didn't try to find out who it was. I was

186

clinging to principles, but I've learned something... Rachel's taught me something. Principles are nothing if they're not combined with compassion and judgement. I had the latter, but not the former. She's changed me, Gabe. And I want her to know that. That's something I haven't told her yet."

Gabe nodded slowly and smiled. "Then go tell her. I can't guarantee what her reaction will be, but looks like you need to tell her."

Zane glanced at the half-open door and could hear the murmur of Rachel's and her father's voices. After tonight, the national news would be full of the changes his tribe had made to their policies, changes Zane had instigated. He followed Gabe out into the hall. "Are you coming?"

"No way. Rachel only invited me to stave off a scene and" —he glanced at the closed door behind which they could hear Jim comforting his daughter—"I reckon I'm too late for that. You go in there and deal with it."

Gabe walked to the door. "Best of luck, mate," he called over his shoulder. "I think you're going to need it!" The door closed with a thunk, leaving Zane alone, half-wishing he could leave with Gabe, leave all the drama and the difficulty behind, but he knew, deep down, he couldn't move forward without facing it.

Zane opened the kitchen door. Rachel was stirring the contents of a pot which sizzled on the stovetop, the steam curling the tendrils of hair which had escaped her ponytail. She glanced at him as he entered, her eyes red and watery.

"Rachel," Zane exclaimed, immediately walking over to her. "I'm so sorry I upset you."

"I should think so," said Jim, standing watching them both. "Now, I'm going to leave you two to sort this out, once and for all."

"Dad! Where are you going?" asked Rachel anxiously,

making Zane's heart sink at her obvious unwillingness to be alone with him.

"None of your business. I'm nearly seventy years old and I think I can go out on my own without your permission." With that, he grabbed his jacket from the hook and left. The backfiring of his old Daimler was the only sound to break the silence which fell over them. Rachel poured the contents of the pot into a bowl, leaving Zane standing, wondering how the hell he was going to break this impasse.

Then he heard a sound and he saw Rachel was crying again. He couldn't hold back any longer and went to her. "Rachel, don't cry. I'm sorry, I thought it would be good news for you."

She flicked the taps on and squirted detergent into the sink, then turned around and put her hands on her hips and he was rewarded with the blackest look he'd seen in a long time. But, even so, he couldn't help thinking she looked hotter than ever.

"You *thought* that, did you? You thought you could block me from seeing my daughter, and then, at a whim, unblock it, and I'd come crawling to you on my knees to give thanks? Is that what you thought? Hey?"

"Of course not. There was no whim—"

"What do you call it when you overturn a decision simply because you discovered it was me? Seems like your principles fly out the window when you want something."

"It's not like that. For Christ's sake, hear me out. There's one reason and one reason only why I've overturned the decision and that's because you made me realize I was wrong." He held up his hand to stop her from interrupting. "You're right, it did involve you, but only because you made me see I hadn't taken everything into consideration."

"You don't say," she said with heavy sarcasm. "The great

Zane forgot to tick a box. And what exactly does this box cover?"

"Compassion. People. Individual circumstances. I judged too soon. I was too swayed by my own history. And I'm sorry about that, Rachel. I'm so sorry for everything I've put you through."

He waited for her to say something but for once her mouth formed no words, only a soft opening 'oh'. She swallowed and bit her lip, suddenly aware of the implications. "You're sorry." She gave a wan smile. "And you think that's enough?"

"I simply mean—"

"I know what you mean!" He suspected that she didn't, but before he could remonstrate, she continued. "And there's nothing simple about it. Anyway, why don't you leave? The party's over before it's begun." She grabbed some saucepans and dropped them into the hot soapy water, gave them a cursory wash before placing them on the drainer.

He glanced around. "Let me help you clear up, at least." That way, he reckoned he might be able to stay and make things feel normal again. "Why don't you sit down and I'll do this?" He grabbed the pot she'd washed from the drying rack, checked it over, and placed it back in the water.

Rachel looked from the pot to Zane. "I've already washed that."

Zane twisted it to show Rachel the smear of food still on it. "It's not clean."

It had seemed a reasonable response from Zane when he uttered the words, but seeing Rachel's face grow angry again, he suddenly realized he'd made a mistake.

"It's not clean? I've washed it and you're going to re-wash it because it's not clean? That's how you carry on, isn't it, Zane? Picking at other people's imperfections, passing judgement on other people's behavior. Nothing ever matches up to your supremely high ideals, does it?"

Zane looked at the pot, complete with the smeared remains of a béchamel sauce, and then back at Rachel, wondering what he'd missed.

"And nothing ever *will*, because you're too damn rigid," she continued. "You have your rules and if something or someone doesn't fit into them, all nice and neat, then you either change them or get rid of them. Well"—she poked him in the chest—"I've got news for you. I'm not going to change, so you may as well leave now."

"*Rachel*, I don't want you to change. That's what I came here to tell you." He paused as he reconsidered his words. "Kind of."

"*Kind* of? You mean you'd *like* to *not* want me to change, but you still *want* me to change, hey?"

"I…" He hesitated, re-running her words in her head, his confusion increasing and his understanding slipping farther out of reach with each re-run. Seemed Etta and Rachel had another thing in common—the ability to confuse him with words.

She stepped closer and folded her arms, her head cocked to one side. "What are you really doing here, Zane? What did you expect my reaction would be to your news?"

He shrugged, turning over the options carefully in his mind before speaking. "I thought you might be pleased."

Her beautiful dark eyebrows shot to the top of her forehead. "Pleased?" She closed her eyes and drew in a deep breath. He couldn't help his eyes descending to her chest which rose and fell with hypnotic power. He managed to lift his gaze before she opened her eyes. "Pleased? Yes, sure, I'm pleased. But what I'm not sure about is whether it changes anything. Does it, Zane?"

The sudden switch from anger to doubt, caught him off-guard. "Maybe." He decided to hedge his bets. "Maybe not."

She rolled her eyes. He'd chosen the wrong response. "Just go," she said.

"No." That was one thing he *was* certain about.

"Then *I* am." She looked down at the pot, irritated. "And put that saucepan down."

He looked down at the pan which he was still holding, scared to move the damn thing anywhere.

"Where?"

Rachel grunted with annoyance, took it from him and, after a moment's hesitation sploshed it into the soapy sink.

"You've put it in the water," he noted with surprise.

"Of course." She looked at him as if he were a dolt. "I don't want to cook using dirty pots."

Baffled, he watched as she vigorously scrubbed the pots and placed them on the drainer. Without glancing at him, she pulled on an oversized cardigan which was hanging on a hook, pulled it around her and went outside.

He followed her down the steps, across the short stretch of lawn until the grass grew patchy and the sand took over. Zane had no idea if she expected him to follow her but, unless he wanted to have another confusing conversation, there was no way he could leave. It was lighter away from the trees and the starlight glanced off the harbor, magnifying the light, lending her silhouette a glow.

She walked up to the end of the short jetty where a couple of chairs still remained from summer. She stopped suddenly and looked up to the sky. By the time he caught up with her he could see the anger had gone, leaving behind only confusion and sadness. His heart broke a little.

"Rachel, are you okay?"

He almost wished for the angry glower to appear on her face again. But it didn't. There was only hurt now. She clutched the chunky cardigan around her. It made her appear more fragile, younger, like a teenager again. Like Etta.

"I don't know *what* I am anymore." She looked up at him and it took him all his control not to scoop her into his arms and keep her safe. But he knew that wouldn't fix anything. Not yet.

"You're still you."

She sat in the chair. "That's what I'm afraid of."

"What? Why should you be afraid of being you?"

She tilted her head until her gaze caught his. "Because I'm not enough, Zane. I'm not enough for *you*, I'm not enough for *me*, and I'm sure as hell not enough for Etta."

She rolled her head back so she was looking straight out to the silver sheen of the harbor.

"Yes, you are. That's why I'm here. That's what I came to tell you."

"You told me. You overturned the decision. The way is clear for me to have a relationship with Etta, providing she wants one. And I think we've established she doesn't."

"Rachel. You only let me tell you part of the story. There's more. Etta has worked hard with her counselor, she's made progress and she's told *her*, and *me*, that she wants to meet with you. She's ready." He reached for her hands which he took in his, willing her to understand with the pressure he applied. "She didn't mean any of those things she said before. She's probably forgotten half of them. It was shock talking. But now... she's ready. All I need to know is whether you are."

She turned slowly back to face him. "Ready? To meet Etta?"

"*Are* you?"

"You mean to say you'll let me and Etta get to know each other?"

"Yes."

"Are you sure she wants to? Are you really sure? Because I don't want to force the situation."

"Yes, I'm sure."

"Right. Right."

The strain in her voice broke down the last shreds of his reserve and he knelt on the jetty and put his arm around her. "Good. I'll make the arrangements."

"Thank you." She sniffed and looked away. "I shouldn't have let it happen. At the time I knew it but somehow I got swept along by all these adults 'knowing' better. I simply went along with it. And I've regretted it every day of my life since. I shouldn't have been away so long. I shouldn't—"

"Hey, stop beating yourself up." He turned her in his arms, and saw the tears pool in her eyes and slide down her cheeks.

She stood up and brushed away her tears. "Look at me, crying! Ridiculous!"

"No, it's not. You lost a baby and now you've found her. That's pretty momentous. I reckon you're allowed a few tears."

"I've found her," she repeated, looking away. "She'll be able to come and visit me…"

"I'll go and get her."

"What?" She reached out for his hand.

"She wants to see you; she knew I was coming here and she's waiting back at the marae."

"Why didn't you tell me?"

"One step at a time."

"I need to change, I need to—"

"Stay here. Don't move, don't change. We'll come to you in ten minutes."

RACHEL WATCHED Zane walk quickly away. She paced one way and then another. She began walking up to the house…

to get what? She didn't know, but a lifetime of resorting to the kitchen in times of grief and happiness, had her entering the kitchen and heating up some milk for hot chocolate. She poured it into a flask and then walked back to the jetty, as Zane had suggested.

She placed the flask and mugs onto the table and sat down, but immediately jumped up again. There was no way she could remain seated, not with Etta about to arrive. Instead, she was pacing when she heard the sound of the car turn into the drive, and park outside. The car lights dimmed and then two car doors slammed and there was silence.

Rachel held her breath. Had she come? *Two* car doors, she reminded herself. *Two*. But no one spoke. Then she heard a rustle of branches being pushed back. She peered into the darkness and saw two shadows—one unmistakably Zane's, the other, shorter and slight. They walked in silence across the grass. She heard the slight scrunch of sand beneath their feet before they emerged onto the jetty. Zane stepped up first.

"Rachel," he said softly. "Etta's here. She'd like to meet you." He paused. "Properly, this time."

Rachel's eyes hadn't left the dark shadow which lurked behind Zane. "Etta?" she asked gently. Etta looked up then and the moonlight caught the whites of her eyes. She looked wide-eyed and nervous. "Etta," she repeated. "Thank you for coming."

Etta nodded, but didn't speak.

"Would you like some hot chocolate? I have some in a flask here." She indicated the table at the end of the jetty, around which wooden chairs were fixed.

Again, a silence which seemed too vast to bridge. Rachel shot Zane a warning glance. She didn't want Etta rushed. She didn't want Zane to prompt her.

"Yeah," said Etta at last. "Please," she added as an afterthought.

"Zane?" Rachel asked.

"Yes, thank you."

Trying to calm her shaking hands, Rachel sat and poured them all a cup, while she spoke, about anything. "We could go inside, but I've always liked to sit outside when I can."

"So do I!" said Etta enthusiastically, without prompting. "I guess we *are* alike, like Uncle Zane says."

Rachel smiled at Zane, who looked from one to the other with satisfaction before sipping the hot chocolate which she knew he didn't like. He managed to hide a grimace.

"Yep. Both strong-willed, stubborn and…"

"And?" prompted Rachel and Etta together.

"Women I would *not* want to be without."

"Just as well we're family then, isn't it?" said Etta. She turned to Rachel, the wide-eyed look replaced by her usual jaunty confidence. "Eh, Mum?"

The night seemed to hold its breath, as Etta's words lingered in the air, and settled somewhere deep inside of Rachel, warming her like no amount of hot chocolate would.

"Yes, it is," Rachel replied.

"Here's to family," Zane said, raising his mug to the others. Rachel and Etta brought theirs to his. "Family," they repeated, clinking their mugs together. He took a drink of the chocolate and grimaced briefly.

"Enjoying the drink, Uncle Zane?" asked Etta with a cheeky grin. "Because I know how much you like hot chocolate!"

Rachel burst out laughing as Zane placed his near full cup onto the table. "I don't know what you two see in it."

"Chocolate!" replied Rachel, as Etta nodded in agreement.

. . .

RACHEL COULDN'T HAVE SAID how long they stayed outside. But the moon had risen high into the sky, when they heard Jim's car return. He followed the sounds of their voices outside and joined them. Rachel brought blankets and more food and drinks outside and they talked. About everything. Polite stuff at first, skirting around issues, then other things, more meaningful things, things which she and her father regretted from the past, things of the future which they wanted to do to make up for it. But all the while, despite the comfortable and uncomfortable things said, there was an understanding which grew. Etta's counselor had done a good job. She'd helped Etta to begin to understand and accept what had happened. And now, Rachel knew, it was up to her to continue to build the relationship, and she couldn't wait.

12

Etta screwed up her face in concentration, as she looked first at the goal, then at the ball, pacing back a half-dozen steps until she had the correct angle. Then she half-ran toward the ball, set in a small mound of earth, and kicked it, her whole body gracefully in tune with the movement, as she twisted into the kick, and the rugby ball went soaring into the air.

Zane ran forward, his whistle in his mouth as they watched the ball rise into the blue sky and then drop down, perfectly placed between the two uprights.

Etta jumped up, fist high in the air.

Zane blew the whistle which signaled the end of the practice.

"Good one, Etta!" said Zane. "You'll play for New Zealand yet."

"Just like my uncle," she said with a grin.

"Yeah, must be. Not like your dad, that's for sure."

"So what's Dad like then?" asked Etta.

"Don't you remember him from his last visit home?"

Etta shot Zane a withering glance as they walked back to the club rooms. "I was only six. All I remember was he had those babies." She scowled.

"Your half-sisters."

"They bawled all the time."

Zane couldn't think of anything to say because his brother's twins *had* cried a lot. They'd been nothing like Etta, who faced everything squarely and bravely, accommodating changes in circumstances as required. Strong and stoic, that was Etta. "True." He glanced at his niece who was covered in mud and had the beginnings of a large bruise on her shin. "And you're more like your mum. She's a force to be reckoned with, too."

"I still don't really understand why she left me."

"No. I don't suppose she does, either. Sometimes, like rugby, people take a mis-step. No one ever does the right thing all the time. It's what comes after that matters. And Rachel's been trying to make up for that mistake, every day of her life, one way or another."

"Do you think she'll stay around here? She says she will, but Aunty reckons she'll be off to the States soon, because they want her over there."

Zane made a mental note to have a word with that particular aunty. There was no skirting the issue now. He took her by the shoulders and faced her. "If Rachel says she will, she will. Ignore the gossips."

"I guess, but…"

"But what?"

"Can't you make sure she stays?"

"And how do you expect me to do that?"

"Marry her."

He nearly choked. "What?"

"Ask her to marry you. Then she'd stay."

"I can't… She wouldn't…"

"You don't know unless you ask and I've seen the way she looks at you."

"What way?"

"You know, Zane. Like all the women do, except when Rachel looks at you like that, you look the same, right back. If *I* can see it, then Rachel would."

"For real?" The shock of being given advice by his ten-year-old niece was making him sound like a teenager.

"Yeah. And it's not only me. All my cousins reckon you're made for each other. But that you'd probably have to grovel lots because that's what men have to do when they've stuffed up as much as you have."

Zane was about to object but closed his mouth instead, knowing Etta was probably right.

"And then there was that stunt you pulled with the photos," added Etta. Zane briefly wondered if all women had this unerring knowledge about how to rub salt into a wound.

"It wasn't a stunt! I—" He suddenly wondered how on earth it was public knowledge. "They know about that?"

"Yeah. Course they do. My cuzzies know everything!" She laughed and went running off.

He was left standing there, wondering how everybody knew everything about his life, knew what he should do, except him. He shook his head and walked across the muddy field to the club rooms, following in Etta's footsteps, suddenly realizing that she could teach him as much as he could teach her.

By the time he reached the club rooms, and the noise of the teams and their families, the heat, steam from the showers mingling with the smell of the food from the kitchen, he knew exactly what he had to do.

~

IT WAS a long drive out to the end of the road where only penguins and seabirds lived. But, as Rachel parked the car on the gravel side of the road, she immediately saw she wasn't the first to arrive. Zane's car was parked around the bend.

Rachel felt the same flutter of nerves and excitement she'd felt when she'd received Zane's text, asking her to meet him. She'd refused the first time, citing a prior engagement. But Zane had persisted and she'd finally agreed to come to this remote spot, as much out of curiosity as anything else.

She stepped out the car, the wind whipping her hair around her face, obscuring her vision, as she pushed the door shut. By the time she'd twisted her hair out the way, Zane had gotten out his car and was looking her way. He stood, hands in his suit trouser pockets, staring at her. It was windier here, close to the open sea. She clamped her hand down to hold her hair as she walked toward him, her thin sandals feeling out the rougher stones on the road where so few cars came.

She stopped a few steps in front of him. "Zane." She cleared her throat and gestured with her hands. "Well, I'm here." She smiled to cover the million and one things which were passing through her head. Had she done something wrong? Had she somehow messed up the fledgling relationship she'd begun with Etta? That magical night on the beach, when Etta had shown to Rachel that she now accepted her as her mother, had only been a month ago, but Rachel had seen Etta regularly and she'd thought things were going well. What if she were wrong?

He smiled briefly. "You are. Thanks for coming." Rachel noted the tension in his face. Something was worrying him. Her nerves ratcheted up a notch.

"Is Etta okay?"

"Etta?" He frowned. "Of course. She's never been better."

Relief flooded her. She exhaled a breath she hadn't known she was holding.

"Why?"

Rachel shrugged. "The sudden text, the strange place to meet, I wondered if I'd…"

"If you'd what?" He shook his head in disbelief. "Done something wrong? Rachel, you've done *everything* right. Etta's changed. She's still the same stroppy headstrong girl, but she's not risking everything to show off, to win anymore. She seems… more content, happier in herself. And that's down to you."

"Me… and the counselor. She's done a great job."

"You both have."

She shrugged, suddenly feeling uncomfortable. "Are we meeting somebody here?"

"No." He didn't elaborate, simply continued to gaze at her with an unreadable expression. "Want to walk?"

"Yes, I guess." She fell into step beside him. "So… why the cloak and dagger stuff?" She tried to smile but her mouth tugged jerkily at the corners. "Zane, tell me, what's going on? What the hell is all this about?"

"I wanted to talk."

"Talk? We can talk in the café. We can talk anywhere. Why bring me all the way out here?"

"Because I wanted to show you something."

She shrugged and opened her arms. "Then show me, and then I can go."

"That's just it." He paused and in that silence a thousand things ran through her brain. "I know the US TV company still want you over there, and I know it's an incredible opportunity for you, but… I don't want you to go."

He hadn't moved toward her. His expression was still unsmiling, but his words were telling her something else. The whole package didn't compute.

"It's not for long."

"How long?"

She shrugged. "I'm not sure. There will be some PR work to do in different locations."

"When's your return flight?"

"It hasn't been booked."

His expression went from unsmiling to grim in an instant. "You're not coming back, are you?"

"Yes, I am. Of *course* I am. There's Etta…"

"Sure. And you know that she'd love nothing better than to get a sporting scholarship to the States."

"Yeah, I know. I thought maybe I could help there."

"By being a resident?"

"I didn't say that."

"You didn't *not* say that."

"Why are you so concerned anyway? It's not like you're going to miss me, surely? I mean, this must be the first time we've been alone together for months."

"I didn't…" He trailed off.

"What? You didn't what?" It wasn't until he turned to her, his eyes shadowed, that she understood. "Really?" she asked. "You didn't think I'd want to be with you? Why?"

He shrugged. "Where to begin?"

"I guess we could begin with the photographs."

"Hey, I'm sorry. You can check with your father, I asked him for permission."

"Is that how you usually carry on business—asking women's fathers for permission?"

"I'm sorry, Rachel. I'm truly sorry. But I really didn't think you'd mind, given what I'd intended them to be used for."

"*Intended* being the operative word."

"It got out of hand. My nieces are hopeless with social media. I'm so sorry."

Rachel had to bite her lip to stop herself from smiling.

"Zane." She reached out and touched him. "You can stop apologizing now. I understand."

His relief was palpable. "You do? Thank God. Because, you know, Rachel, I'd never do anything to hurt you. I hate that you think I'm like the other men in your life. I—"

"I *know* you're not. Not least because they've never said 'sorry' to me as many times as you… if ever."

He exhaled roughly with relief. "Right. Good. So…"

She cocked her head to one side to catch his gaze. "So?"

"So… I wanted to say… about your one-way ticket."

"Yes?"

"That I wish it were a two-way ticket."

"Do you really think I still intend to leave here?"

His shrug told her that that was exactly what he believed.

"You do!"

"Of course I do," he said. He walked toward her then and she could see the struggle which was going on beneath the surface. "And I don't want you to go."

"You don't?" They'd hardly spent any time alone together over the past few months. They were both so busy and then there was Etta. They both wanted to include her in their lives as much as possible. But it had allowed Rachel to doubt Zane's feelings for her. And she wanted to know, now, finally. She took a deep breath. "And why's that? Etta?"

"That's one reason. But there are others."

"I'm listening."

"I owe you."

"Owe me what?"

"Owe you for preventing you from finding Etta."

"But you didn't know it was me."

"True. But I didn't try to find out who it was, or anything behind the application. I passed judgement without knowing the full story. And I want to try to make that up to you."

"You have already. By helping me and Etta reunite. I can't

believe how well we get on, compared to only a few short months ago."

"But there's more." He reached out and took hold of her hand. She closed her eyes. "Zane, let me go."

"No. I can't. Rachel, hear me out." He walked around until he was facing her. "I haven't finished my list of reasons you should stay."

"I only needed that one. Etta."

"I have some back up reasons—three in total."

"You don't need them."

"I think I do. I think I need to tell you that I don't want you to leave...*me*. I can't imagine this place without you. I know we haven't known each other long, Rachel, but I don't want you to go. I want you to be with me, to work alongside me with Etta, to do it together. Do you understand what I'm saying?"

She shook her head. She daren't understand.

"I'm saying that I love you. For the first time in my life I'm in love and I've been too stupid to see it. I don't want you to go, because pure and simple, I want you at my side. Rachel?"

But she couldn't speak and he pulled her against his chest where she rested her cheek and sighed.

"What's the third?" she murmured.

"Third?" he asked, puzzled, as he pushed her hair from her face. "Third what?"

"Third reason you want me to stay. You said there were three."

He huffed lightly and stepped away, his hand firmly clasping hers and gestured around the place. "It's all of this. It's this place, my home, your home. Look around. This is where you were raised, this is where I was raised. What better place for us to raise our children?"

"Children?" she repeated faintly.

"Our family's children. Etta, my nieces and nephews, Gabe's kids, Amber's kids which no doubt she'll have lots of. And... I hope one day, our own children. Rachel, please don't go."

She half-laughed, half-cried. "Let's get this straight. You're offering me a chance with my daughter I've been longing for my whole life, the chance to live close to the family I love, and a chance..." She faltered and took a deep breath and looked up at him. "To be with the man who won't stay out of my mind."

"I'm in your mind?"

"And everywhere else, too."

"Everywhere?" he said, his features relaxing into a definitely satisfied macho expression. "Maybe we'd better leave this place and go somewhere where I can make sure I'm everywhere."

"That, Zane Black, is a very suggestive comment. And also a very good one."

He grinned as they walked back to their cars. "Trouble is, Rachel, your place or mine? Either place will be full of family."

"Christchurch, then. A motel, I think. One night away."

He stopped short. "Will you marry me, Rachel? As soon as possible?"

"What's the urgency?"

"Because I love you—heart and soul—and I don't ever want to be parted from you. And... I want more than one night in a motel. I want night after night with you, day after day, and I don't want to be apart from my family, our people. Will you?"

"Yes, oh, yes, Zane!"

The world spun around them as they kissed. When they parted he withdrew something from his pocket.

"What's this?" She laughed. "Don't tell me you have a ring."

He smiled and let it unravel. At the end of a strand of leather was a large greenstone pendant. "I want you to have this."

"That's your grandmother's, isn't it?"

"Yes, it's one of our tribe's *taonga*. That's Maori for treasure," he added.

Rachel took it, and caressed the smooth cool greenstone —*pounamu*, jade. Whatever you called it, it was one of Maori's treasures from their history and a part of their culture. "It's beautiful."

"It belonged to my grandmother, and I want you to have it. *She* wants you to have it."

"I can't! I mean it's part of your family's culture, your people. You can't give it to me."

"It's a part of me. You have my treasure, you have my heart, they're both yours, to do with what you wish. I just need to give them to you, the rest is up to you. I'll never force you to do anything. It's up to you, whether you leave or stay."

"Zane! I'm not leaving! Well, only for a few weeks. And then I'll be back. There's no way I'm choosing any kind of career over what I have here. Besides..." She smiled. "I can have my cake and eat it... quite literally. My ticket might be open-ended because we're not sure of what's required when we get over there. But I will be back. We're going to be filming *here*, not over there."

"Here?"

"Yes, at Belendroit. It's the perfect place. It's home, after all."

He kissed her then. Then he withdrew another package from his pocket, a velvet box inside of which was a diamond ring. "Will you take it? Will you be my wife?"

"Zane, I think I loved you the moment I set eyes on you. Definitely the second moment." She grinned. "I will." And they kissed, his arms enveloping her in an embrace as if he never wanted to let her go. And she never wanted to be let go.

13

Four weeks later...

It couldn't be nerves, Rachel thought, as her father's ancient Daimler turned into the church driveway and parked outside, beside the gardens where craft markets were held on Saturdays. No, far more likely to be the smell of petrol combined with leather that made her feel so queasy. She'd been worried it wouldn't get them here, but hadn't the heart to refuse her father's offer of bringing her to the church in his beloved old car.

She ducked her head to look out the window at the nineteenth-century wooden church with its gray roof, white weatherboards, and peaked-roofed porch. Behind the church, native bush rose up the hill, making the church appear nestled and cozy, unchanged over the century and more it had been in existence.

She turned to look in the back seat where Etta was already fingering the door handle, waiting for Rachel to give the signal. "Are you okay?" asked Rachel.

"Yeah, sure." Etta didn't look in the least bit nervous,

despite her initial unwillingness to be a bridesmaid—something that sounded far too girly for her. But after negotiations over the dress (no frills and not white) and over the hair (no flowers stuck in it), she was on board. Rachel let her gaze settle on her for a few seconds. Etta's hair, for once, wasn't pulled back into a ponytail, but fell in natural soft waves, framing her face and falling down her back. The unformed softness around Etta's cheeks was already beginning to take the shape of a beautiful young woman. And Rachel knew, without a doubt, that when Etta became that woman, Rachel would still be a part of her life. Etta gave Rachel a quick impatient glance, followed by a swift smile. She was mercurial, a wild child who would only be tamed by her own fierce brand of love. "Ready, Mum?"

Rachel didn't think she'd ever tire of hearing herself called 'Mum'. "Ready."

The organ music spilled out the porch of the old church and down the steps, across the grass to where they stepped out of her father's ancient Daimler.

An usher waiting on the step, grinned at them, and indicated to someone inside that they'd arrived—suitably late, thanks to her father's refusal to drive the Daimler at a reasonable speed, so he could wave and chat to passing locals.

"Ready?" Jim was beaming broadly as he offered his arm to her, not so much oblivious to the fact they were late, but relishing the dramatic entrance it would bring.

"More than." She grinned back as she slipped her arm through his. Etta collected the flowing skirt of Rachel's cream gown and held it high, as she'd been shown by her aunties who were waiting inside, and they walked into the church. The smell of polish and flowers and incense and old wood surrounded them, and filled Rachel with a sudden rush of nerves. "Dad!" she whispered.

"What is it, darling? Not nerves, surely?"

She swallowed and nodded, unable to utter a single word. It wasn't butterflies in her stomach but a horde of rampaging elephants. Her hands were shaking around her bouquet—roses from Belendroit's garden, in all shades of pink. She'd been on TV, presented shows to live audiences many times, but she'd never done anything as nerve-racking as this.

"You have nothing to worry about. You have a man who adores you waiting inside, and"—he glanced behind at Etta, who stood tall in her floor length red satin dress—"and a daughter who will be there every step of the way, supporting you. You've nothing to worry about," he repeated, his eyes filling with teary love. "And you look utterly beautiful," Jim said, kissing her cheek. "Just like your mother. She'd have loved to have been here. To have seen you so happy. And with…" He couldn't finish the sentence. They both blinked back the tears.

"Don't get me going, Dad," she said, sweeping her finger under her eyes.

"I'm sorry." The church organ pounded out the chords of the Wedding March. "That's our cue, my darling, let's do this."

They walked up to the arch where the whole church was in view, and paused as every face turned to them. The whole of the church's interior seemed to glow. The wooden walls of the church were bright with the warm radiance of candles, and people's faces reflected, or emanated, the same kind of radiance—one of love. Rachel couldn't see Zane and Gabe—his best man—as they were hidden behind bobbing heads, and flashing cameras. There were so many people here, and she knew them all.

She smiled as she caught different people's gazes. Her family: Max and Laura, Amber wearing something bright and exotic, her elder sister Lizzi and Pete and their daughter,

Aimee. Even her elusive brothers Rob and Cameron had showed up, tanned from goodness knows what continent they'd been traveling on. Zane's family was everywhere. His grandmother sat at the front, dignified and commanding as always.

Rachel glanced behind her at Etta, who, faced with the entire congregation, looked suddenly nervous. Rachel smiled encouragement and Etta grinned back. A 'let's just get on with this' kind of grin. Then the photographers and people moved aside, allowing a clear view up the aisle to where Zane waited with Gabe. And from that moment, there was no one else. Rachel's nerves vanished but she could see Zane was nervous and the knowledge gave her confidence.

There was a murmur from people as she walked past, but she didn't hear them. She kept her eyes on the one sure thing that kept her steady, that gaze that had kept her moving forward, since the day she'd first seen it. Zane's gaze, his eyes —Zane, willing her on to him, Zane's love keeping her safe like a treasure.

When she reached him he whispered in her ear, "I like your necklace."

She glanced down at the jade necklace and touched it with her forefinger. Then she looked up at him. "Me, too. I'll treasure it, always."

A discreet cough from the priest made them turn around and he began to speak. The words of the ceremony felt weighted with meaning. Before today they'd been merely words, but now, with Zane beside her, his eyes fixed on hers, and his hands holding hers tightly, she understood every nuance, every syllable of them. With the last of the responses uttered, she lifted her face to Zane's and he kissed her.

The forgotten congregation roared their approval. The sound echoed around the old colonial church as everyone rose and began to applaud. Above it all, the sound of a Maori *waiata* rose—an ancient song sung by the whole of Zane's whanau about love, respect and family. They walked back down the aisle where now people moved, offering them congratulations and kisses.

Eventually they emerged from the church into the bright sunlight and looked out to the blue harbor, golden hills above, and to the blue sky daubed with fluffy white clouds. Rachel looked around, searching for one pair of eyes, cheeky eyes—*her* eyes—and found them. She'd done what Zane had suggested, taking one day at a time, one step at a time, so slowly that she hardly noticed the imperceptible daily changes. But now, as she looked at Etta, her daughter, laughing with her friends, throwing clouds of confetti over Zane and her, all smiles, just for Rachel, she realized exactly how far they'd come. And they had still further to go and, with Zane at her side, Rachel couldn't wait.

Yep, she thought, as Zane's arm tightened around her waist, she was in the right place. She was home.

GABE STOOD a little apart from the newly married couple, beside Amber.

"What is it with this family?" asked Amber. "They're getting married at a rate of one per year. It'll be you next."

"Me?" He huffed. "Not likely. I'm fine as I am." He glanced at his red-headed little sister, dressed in bright colors, with flowers in her hair. She marched to the beat of a different drum. "It'll be more likely you."

She smiled a far-away smile. "Marriage? No way. But if a long-haired poet with dreamy eyes and hair—a little bit too long, perhaps—comes walking along, a guitar slung over his shoulder, then I'm open to offers." She gave him a disarming grin. "Come on, I've bags of heart-shaped confetti to throw at the happy couple." She handed Gabe a bag and they proceeded to deluge Rachel and Zane.

Gabe stood beside Zane as the family grouped together for a photograph in front of the church. It took a while to settle everyone. Long enough for an ache to settle in Gabe's heart as he watched his beautiful sister put her arm around her daughter and gaze lovingly up to her new husband. The photographer snapped the photo, immortalizing Gabe's love for his sister and his own empty heart forever.

EPILOGUE

Twelve months later...

Zane stretched across the crispy white linen on the tablecloth and held up his glass of beer to Rachel's champagne flute. "Happy anniversary, Mrs. Black!"

Rachel clinked his glass with hers. "Happy anniversary, Mr. Black. What a year!"

He placed his glass on the silver coaster and took her hand in both of his. "The best year. I mean, *the* best year."

"Best, and most difficult, and most rewarding, and most joyful. Most everything, really."

"I guess it's better to have something of everything rather than a lot of nothing."

"Yeah, 'nothing' is very over-rated. I did nothing for ten years."

"Come on! You built a career—a career which is still going well."

"True." She smiled. "A bit of re-branding and voila! A family show—"

"Syndicated around the world."

There was a subtle cough from behind Rachel. "Excuse me, would you care for a starter? It's a twist of seafood with avocado on a bed of puha... I mean watercress."

"Strictly speaking," said Rachel, "puha and watercress are two different vegetables."

Zane grinned and raised an eyebrow. "Maori kai, eh? Fusion food—Maori-European."

The waitress shrugged, her face a study of seriousness. "That's correct, sir."

"Then count me in."

The slender, dark-eyed waitress carefully placed the unusual starter on the table and stepped away.

Rachel heard a giggle come from behind her but she didn't turn around. The view in front of her—Zane, tanned, handsome in a white shirt, his suit jacket having quickly been hooked on the back of his chair, as it was too hot in the evening sun—was too mesmerizing to take her gaze from. Twelve months with this man who'd barely left her side, fifty-two weeks with someone who'd proved his love every single day as her husband. She could still scarcely believe it.

She took a bite of the food. "Um, tender and tasty, a fine starter." She gave a thumbs-up to the waitress who grinned at the sign of approval. "Although... maybe a little lemon juice. What do you think, Zane?"

"It's fine as it is." Typical Zane—he ate with relish without any thought to its subtleties. He'd half-finished it already. She didn't think she'd ever really educate his taste buds into fine dining. "But you're the expert." He looked over to the waitress. "A little lemon juice for my wife, please."

The waitress scowled and muttered something to another waiter—dressed in black trousers, which were too large for him, and a white shirt which had seen better days—who stood next to her, and punched him on the arm. "I told you not to forget the lemon."

"We haven't got any," the boy complained.

"What's that, then?" the waitress asked, pointing to a lemon tree which grew by the steps of the small deck on which Zane and Rachel were eating. She punched him again for good measure. This time Zane noticed.

Zane frowned. "Etta! What have I told you about punching people?"

"To only do it if they deserve it," she muttered, as she pulled a lemon off the tree. She stabbed a knife into it and cut off a chunk on the preparation table to one side, where the anniversary feast had been prepared. Etta took a deep breath and walked over to Rachel again. "Lemon juice, Mum, I mean madam, I mean Rachel, I mean Mum."

"Thank you." Rachel watched as Etta carefully squeezed the chunky slice over her starter. Rachel jumped as a stray squirt sprayed her cheek. She quickly brushed it away and returned Zane's grin.

"You're welcome." Etta looked up into Rachel's eyes. "I did it just like you showed me at Belendroit. Just like you did on TV."

Rachel reached out and squeezed the young hand in hers. "You did. You wait, you'll be the next TV star in the family."

"No way. I'm going to play international rugby." Etta grinned, and was shouting at her cousin to bring out the next course when a rugby ball whacked against the deck. She looked up sharply, yelled at the kid who'd booted the ball and ran out, tucked it under her arm, and ran off.

Rachel's eyes lingered on Etta as she out-ran a group of boys across the marae and out into the open hills. Her girl.

Zane followed her gaze. "She's getting there, Rachel. You've both come a long way."

"And sometimes I feel there's a long way to go."

"You've got a lifetime to get there. But, you know, you're both doing fine."

They looked over to their families. Jim was talking to Zane's grandmother—having overcome their decade-old feud, they were now chatting like old friends. Amber was also there, working on some Maori crafts with Zane's cousins.

"Where's Gabe? I thought he said he'd be here tonight."

Rachel shrugged. "I don't know. It's not like him to refuse a free hangi."

"Maybe something's come up."

She shrugged. "He doesn't usually have any problem getting a locum to cover for him."

"Then maybe he's out on a date."

"Gabe? You're kidding. He's hopeless with women. He's holding out for some special woman who doesn't exist."

"You don't know that."

"True. But that appears to be exactly what he's doing. I simply want him to be happy."

"He will be. You'll see. He just has to find someone. You never know, maybe he's found someone already."

"Yeah, right." Rachel suddenly twisted uncomfortably in her chair. "Gabe needs to hurry up. I want our little one"—she rubbed her pregnant stomach—"to be raised surrounded by cousins."

"No worries there, my love. Look around."

Etta suddenly emerged, dusted herself off and took on the role of waitress which she'd insisted on as her present to her uncle and mum. She cleared the plates away and placed the main hangi course in front of them. While the rest of the family and whanau were eating in the marae, seated together, the deck around Zane and Rachel had been kitted out like a first-class restaurant in honor of their anniversary dinner.

Etta held up the pepper grinder. "Would Mum, I mean madam, care for some pepper on her lamb?"

"I would."

Etta carefully ground a dusting onto Rachel's dinner. "Is that enough?"

Zane and Rachel grinned as Etta swatted away her helper who was lurking with the salt. "That's perfect," said Rachel.

And it was.

~

Dear Reader,

Thank you for reading *Yours to Treasure*, the second in my **Lantern Bay** series. I hope you enjoyed it! Reviews are always welcome—they help me and they help prospective readers decide if they'd enjoy the book.

The next book in the series is *Yours to Cherish*, featuring Gabe and Madeleine.

If you're new to my books and would like to know more about some of the characters you've met in *Yours to Give* and *Yours to Treasure*, why not check out my **Mackenzies** series? The last book in the series, Summer at the Lakehouse Café, features Lizzi and Pete.

Happy reading!

Sophie

YOURS TO CHERISH

BOOK 3, LANTERN BAY—GABE AND MADELEINE

Archaeologist Madeleine MacGillivray arrives in Akaroa with a backpack and a story she refuses to tell. Mysterious women are a weakness of Dr Gabriel Connelly's—especially if they're beautiful. But, despite an undeniable chemistry, Madeleine insists on

remaining friends only. However, Gabe has six months in which to change her mind; six months in which to unlock the mystery surrounding the lovely, mysterious Madeleine. But, after he discovers the truth, will he wish he hadn't?

EXCERPT

Gabe followed the dogs around the corner. Maddy was walking up the path from the beach but hadn't yet seen him. Despite the time they'd spent together, she was still an enigma. She had the looks of a supermodel, the brains of a university professor, and the shy, delicate, untrusting heart of a beaten dog. He didn't understand her, but he would. He never gave up on a beaten dog. He reached down and petted the two cocker spaniels—Stanley and Boo—who were most definitely not beaten, but instead, thoroughly spoiled.

"Come on, you two." He looked up just as Maddy saw him. "Let's go and meet our mysterious guest."

They barked in agreement and trotted happily at his side as he walked down the lawn to where the grass turned into the sandy beach.

He stopped and petted the dogs but didn't take his eyes off her. She looked different and, as she came nearer, he realized why. She was wearing a dress. It was the first time he'd seen her in anything but shorts and a shirt. The dress was neither new nor smart, but its vintage material draped around her long, lean body, and drifted aside with each step she took. And it was covered with flowers. Old-fashioned pink roses with trailing green stems and leaves.

"Maddy," he said, trying, without success, to suppress a grin that he knew his siblings would have described as silly.

She gave him a wary smile. "Gabriel," she said, before giving her attention to the two affectionate dogs who jumped around her, licking her hands and ankles. Gabe understood their impulse. It was all he could do not to press his lips to her uncertain ones, and coax them into certainty. Instead, he thrust his hands into his pockets to ensure he didn't reach out to her, and formed his lips into a smile, rather than a kiss.

"Only my brother, Jonny, used to call me that."

Her wary smile faltered once more, and she glanced away. But when she looked back at him, the smile had returned, firmer than before, as if she'd made a decision. "I like it. It suits you."

They fell into step, the dogs bounding around them. As they turned a corner, Belendroit came into view, and she stopped abruptly.

"What's the matter?" he asked.

She shook her head. "It's just as I'd imagined."

He frowned. "You've imagined this place?"

"Yes."

"What, since I invited you here?"

She shook her head but didn't elaborate. Instead, she bent down and fussed over Boo, who was looking particularly beautiful with her adoring expression, and golden coat gleaming in the late afternoon sun.

He shrugged and decided to take a stab at the answer himself. "I guess it looks intriguing from the Backpackers. What with the lanterns always lit—day and night."

"Why is that?"

"It's an old family tradition which my mother insisted on continuing. Guiding lights for her family's safe return home."

He looked from the house back to her. The expression in her eyes was strange, unreadable, as if she were miles away, looking at him with new eyes. A shiver tracked down his spine. It was as if someone had walked over his grave. Even the two dogs, Stanley and Boo, had picked up on the atmosphere and Stanley, the more sensitive of the two, nudged his head against Maddy's knee as if providing comfort. While Boo, always keen to move on when things became too soppy, found a half-chewed ball and dropped it at Gabe's feet.

Glad of the interruption, Gabe picked up the ball and threw it toward the house. He was off with his aim, and it knocked over a pot, sending the flowers, earth, and terra-cotta shards everywhere. There were shrieks, a few choice words from his sisters, and a bellowing shout from his father.

Gabe shot Maddy a rueful glance. "Welcome to my family."

ALSO BY SOPHIE HAYDON

The Mackenzies

SOPHIE HAYDON

Lantern Bay

Yours to Give

Yours to Treasure

Yours to Cherish

Yours to Keep

Yours Forever

Yours to Love

www.ingramcontent.com/pod-product-compliance
Lightning Source LLC
Chambersburg PA
CBHW030113260626
47156CB00008B/2635